"No! No way." Thumpa-thumpa-thumpa *went her heart. "I told you earlier that I am not accepting your proposal."*

"Relax, Rebecca. I'm not proposing." Seth sighed the sigh of a hurt man. She didn't buy it for a second. "I do have some pride, you know."

Not proposing? "But you're kneeling."

"I am." He tugged at the laces on her left sneaker. "I'm tying your shoe, before you fall and I have to spend the night pacing in the hospital, worrying if you and our baby are okay."

"Oh." She took that in and shrugged in feigned indifference. "Well, then. Go ahead."

"Besides which," he said in an irritatingly cheerful manner, "you'll be proposing to me soon enough. And when you do, Rebecca, I promise you that I will say yes."

Dear Reader,

There are many instances throughout our lives that symbolize new beginnings: certain holidays, the start of each year, graduations, new jobs, falling in love, weddings and of course—the birth of a baby.

Usually these moments are filled with excitement and anticipation for what the future will bring. Sometimes, though, our happiness and hope give way to the crushing weight of fear. Fear can stop us in our tracks. Fear can make us back away from almost anything—even something as wondrous and miraculous as love.

In this book, *An Officer, a Baby and a Bride,* you'll meet Rebecca, a woman who has allowed fear to form her decisions, to disastrous results, and Seth, a military man who has never been afraid of anything...until he's faced with losing the woman and the child he loves.

At its heart, this story is about courage. Seth and Rebecca will not only have to fight their individual demons, but they'll have to find a way to move beyond them in order to claim the future that fate has planned.

Every book I write holds a special place in my heart, but this story is one of my favorites. I hope it becomes one of yours, as well.

Enjoy!

Tracy Madison

AN OFFICER, A BABY AND A BRIDE

TRACY MADISON

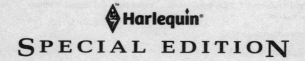
Harlequin®

SPECIAL EDITION

Recycling programs
for this product may
not exist in your area.

ISBN-13: 978-0-373-65677-6

AN OFFICER, A BABY AND A BRIDE

Copyright © 2012 by Tracy Leigh Ritts

Printed in U.S.A.

Books by Tracy Madison

Harlequin Special Edition

*Miracle Under the Mistletoe #2154
*A Match Made by Cupid #2170
*An Officer, a Baby and a Bride #2195

*The Foster Brothers

Other titles by Tracy Madison available in ebook format.

TRACY MADISON

lives in northwestern Ohio with her husband, four children, one bear-size dog, one loving-but-paranoid pooch and a couple of snobby cats. Her house is often hectic, noisy and filled to the brim with laugh-out-loud moments. Many of these incidents fire up her imagination to create the interesting, realistic and intrinsically funny characters that live in her stories. Tracy loves to hear from readers. You can reach her at tracy@tracymadison.com.

To my father: for bringing me Zero candy bars home
from work, taking me on motorcycle rides
and chasing down an ice cream truck for me.
Thank you, Dad, for all the ways you show your love.

Chapter One

Children's voices, bright and happy, punctuated the late afternoon. Several houses down, a lawn mower rumbled its distinctive hum. The breeze carried the light perfume of flowers along with the appetizing scents of charcoal and grilled burgers. Cars drove by, leaves rustled and birds chirped. In all ways, the street was alive with the normal sounds and smells of spring.

Normalcy, Captain Seth Foster thought, *was a type of heaven that most folks never really considered.* Well, most civilians. He, on the other hand, had given the idea of normalcy a great deal of thought throughout his deployment in Afghanistan.

He'd returned to the States less than a week ago, and today, Seth had driven to his parents' house in Portland, Oregon, for an extended leave. Four weeks of rest lay in front of him. His plan for every day of those four weeks was to engage in completely normal activities.

Activities such as eating a home-cooked meal with his family, verbally sparring with his two older brothers, reconnecting with his parents and now, sitting on the front porch of the Victorian home he'd grown up in, enjoying a beer with the company of his brothers.

Seth had anticipated this moment, this exact second in time, when life would—for a little while, at least—become ordinary again.

Of course, he hadn't anticipated that his lamebrained brother had been keeping a secret for months. Or that Jace would choose this moment to reveal that secret, and in doing so, dispel all of Seth's plans for a normal visit home.

Seth took a long draw from his beer before settling his gaze on Jace, the middle brother in the Foster clan. Their older brother, Grady, seemed as shocked by Jace's disclosure as Seth was but had wisely kept his mouth shut—though he hadn't left his brothers alone to battle it out. Nah, he'd stay put and watch over them, ready to jump in if what followed took a nasty turn.

Keeping his attention on Jace, Seth said, "I'm not going to kill him, Grady. Even if I was so inclined, the Air Force doesn't take kindly to fratricide."

"I figured that much." Grady stretched out his long legs. "Still, think I'll sit right here for a while. Enjoy my beer."

"I'm not going to hit him, either."

"I would." Grady's tenor was flat. "If he kept that type of news away from me."

Jace cleared his throat. "If either of you want to clock me across the jaw, go for it. But you should know I'd make the same choice today under the same circumstances."

The temper that Seth had managed to contain flared into being. "Watch it, bro, or I might take you up on that." God, he still couldn't wrap his mind around Jace's announcement.

"You're one hundred percent in this? There is zero doubt that Rebecca is pregnant?"

"I'm certain." Jace raked his fingers through his shaggy black hair. "I wasn't when I originally met with her. Which is partly why I didn't tell you then."

Seth remembered asking Jace to look in on Rebecca Carmichael, a woman he'd corresponded with for nearly a year before their meeting the prior October. He'd been given a short leave from active duty to recoup from an ill-fated mission. After attending a funeral, he spent his time here, in Portland. It had taken several phone conversations, but Rebecca had finally agreed to meet for coffee.

Closing his eyes for a millisecond, Seth savored the taste of the icy-cold microbrew. Coffee became dinner, which turned into drinks, which then became a weekend Seth would never forget. When he returned to duty, his goals for the future—which had always been absolute—shifted into something different than he'd ever seen for himself. A future he hoped might include Rebecca. He'd been all set to take it slow, to keep their relationship on the easy and familiar ground on which it had started, when Rebecca stopped writing. Concerned, he tried reaching her by phone, only to find her number disconnected.

This remained the status quo until sometime in January, when Seth emailed Jace and asked him to ascertain that Rebecca was okay. Jace's response that Rebecca was fine, that her life had been busy but she would get in touch when she could, eased Seth's worry. When another month passed without a peep, Seth figured that was Rebecca's way of saying goodbye.

He'd written her once more, wished her well and focused on the day to day. Every now and then his thoughts would return to her, to the future he'd barely glimpsed before it dissolved into dust. For the most part, though, Seth had pushed Rebecca out of his mind.

Until now. Until faced with the possibility that she was pregnant with *his* child.

"How do you know for certain?" Seth asked, picking up the conversation where Jace had left off. "Have you talked to her again? Seen her?"

"I haven't, but…a friend kept tabs on her." Jace spoke quickly, as if worried Seth would interrupt him. "I know she's pregnant. What I don't know is who the father is."

"What friend? You didn't involve Olivia or Melanie in this, did you?" Grady asked, speaking of his wife and Jace's fiancée.

"If I'd told Olivia, I might as well have told you," Jace shot back. "And you'd have gone to Seth right away, which is what I was trying to avoid. Nor did I tell Melanie. She wouldn't have approved of what she would describe as my… ah…kinglike attitude."

Grady chuckled. "She's called you out on that a few times already, hasn't she?"

"You're one to talk." Jace glowered at Grady. "Because talking Olivia into dating you instead of giving her the divorce she wanted was so *un*kinglike."

Grady shrugged, apparently not bothered by Jace's statement. "We didn't get divorced, so I'd say my methods worked fine. Besides, what happens between…"

Frustration roared through Seth's blood. On a different day, he'd love to hear every detail of his brother and sister-in-law's reconciliation. The couple had separated after their five-year-old son Cody had died in a tragic car accident. A drunk driver had lost control of his vehicle and smashed into Grady's, killing the boy almost instantly.

It had been a horrible time for all of them. Seth hadn't believed that Grady and Olivia would be able to move beyond such an all-encompassing pain. Somehow, though, they had. He was happy for them. And when he learned Olivia was expecting a baby in August, now only a few months away, he'd been even happier.

Now, though, he wanted to hear about Rebecca and the baby *she* carried.

"*How* did your friend keep tabs on Rebecca, Jace?" Seth asked, dragging his brother's attention back to the current topic of conversation.

"It's like this… I hired an investigator friend of mine to—"

"You hired a P.I. to spy on Rebecca?" Seth was three seconds away from leaping out of his chair and strangling his brother. "A little overkill, don't you think?"

"All he did was employ Rebecca as his accountant and set up monthly appointments to see how she was doing. He didn't *spy* on her." Jace pulled in a breath. "Look, if she needed something, I wanted to know. But no one followed her around or snapped pictures of her."

"So you hired a P.I. to spy on her," Seth repeated, his anger growing by the second. "Whether he saw her once a month or sat in front of her house every damn night, his goal was to retrieve information in a covert manner. Is that correct?"

"Okay, yes." Jace planted his elbows on his knees. "I know it was wrong, but I wanted to be in a position to help if she needed anything. I swear, Seth, my intentions were honorable."

Seth gave a short nod, hearing the truth in his brother's words. "You realize that you wouldn't have had to go to such lengths if you'd shared your suspicions up front? Dammit, Jace! If she is carrying my baby, I had a right to know the second you thought that was a possibility."

"Why?" Jace countered, his eyes unflinching. "She wasn't responding to your emails or letters. You couldn't reach her by phone. There was nothing you could do."

"I would've liked the opportunity to try." Seth swore again. "I'm working real hard here to keep my temper in check, but you're making that difficult. We're brothers. We're supposed to look out for each other, so for the life of me, I cannot comprehend—"

"What do you think I was doing? I knew you'd be ticked." Jace gave a tired shake of his head. "But I *was* looking out for you. My goal was to protect you."

"Protect me?" Seth said, his voice dangerously soft as he deduced what Jace was getting at. "You believed I wouldn't be able to do my job safely if I knew Rebecca might be pregnant with my child? Am I getting this right?"

Seth's job, as a pilot in the Air Force, typically didn't carry that much risk. And while his deployment to Afghanistan, where he was part of a planning cell, had placed him in a few precarious situations, his role there had also been relatively safe. Even so, his family worried.

"I wanted you to come home safe." Jace's jaw set in the stubborn line all Foster men were known for. "So yeah, bro, I decided to wait until you were here to tell you. So you could focus on facts and not what-ifs. Why is that so wrong?"

"Because it was an idiotic move," Grady said without rancor. "Imagine if I knew something about Melanie that involved you and I kept that away from you?"

"That's an idiotic statement," Jace retorted, also without rancor. "I'm here. I have the ability to go to Melanie and deal with whatever you might have discovered. Seth *wasn't* here. Seth was in Afghanistan, doing God knows what." He set pleading eyes upon Seth. "I worried about you nonstop. This family can't take another loss."

Jace was referring to Cody and the pain everyone in their family had gone through, still went through. If there was one thing Seth would change if he had the power, it would be the senseless death of his nephew. The fiercest edge of his anger receded. He didn't agree with Jace's decisions, but he understood his brother's motivation.

"I get it," Seth said with a sigh. "However, you went about it the wrong way. I have been trained to focus on the job, on the objective of any given mission. Emotions do not, cannot, interfere when you're on the job."

"Look, you're my baby brother," Jace said. "I'll always want to protect you. I can't apologize for that, but I'm sorry for upsetting you."

Well, that was considerably more than Seth figured he'd get. He remained frustrated with Jace, and he was drowning in the knowledge that he might have a child coming into this world. How could Rebecca keep that away from him?

The possibility existed the baby wasn't his, and that was why Rebecca had stopped communicating. On a logical level, that scenario made the most sense. But his ramped-up intuition and the facts of that weekend told a different story. Even without those facts, Seth had learned years ago to trust his instincts. He wasn't about to stop now.

Clenching and unclenching his empty hand, he considered if he should push the subject with Jace. Why, though? Wasting minutes arguing wasn't the smartest use of Seth's time. A better use would be deciding how to proceed.

In any mission, the first step was gathering all of the necessary intel. Only then could the following steps be planned and executed with success.

"Fair enough," he said in a controlled manner. "I'll set your misguided actions aside because you're my brother and I believe you were operating with good intentions." Seth finished his beer, waited a beat and said, "Tell me everything you know."

If a room could be a living, breathing entity, then this room had devoured hundreds of stuffed pink teddy bears, swallowed several dozen bottles of Pepto-Bismol and then spewed all of it out in a massive spray of pink. There were pink streamers, pink balloons, pink plates, pink glasses, pink napkins in pink napkin holders and pink flowers. Not to mention the multitudes of little pink cakes and pastries, which the guests could wash down with pink punch that had pink ice cubes frozen in the shapes of tiny baby feet and baby rattles.

In other words: a major overabundance of pink.

Rebecca Carmichael rubbed her swollen belly while holding back a groan. Her unborn daughter responded with a flurry of miniature kung fu kicks, as if expressing her profound agreement with her mother's silent assessment.

Yes, definitely too much pink.

Rebecca could only blame herself. If she'd gotten out of bed earlier, she could have helped Jocelyn decorate, and by doing so, limited the explosion of color that had overtaken her earth-toned living room. But she'd slept in and her sister had taken full advantage.

Planting her hands on her hips, Rebecca spun in a slow circle, taking in the entire spectacle. Maybe she could get away with pulling down a few of the *Congratulations! It's a Girl!* banners, along with a good handful or two of the streamers.

Except the last thing she wanted was to hurt her sister's feelings. Jocelyn had put considerable effort into planning today, and the baby shower was important to her.

"What do you think, kid?" Rebecca asked her rounded belly. "Will your aunt notice if a few of her decorations go missing?"

Before her brilliant daughter—because of course, she would prove to be brilliant—had a chance to respond, the familiar sound of Rebecca's mother and sister arguing floated from the kitchen. Now what? When Allison and Jocelyn got into it, they could keep going for hours.

Resigned to playing peacemaker, Rebecca trudged toward the kitchen. Jocelyn was only twenty-two, seven years younger than Rebecca, and hadn't yet learned to pick her battles with their mother. Allison Carmichael, as much as Rebecca loved her, was the type of mother that completely took to heart the saying, "Mother knows best," even when she didn't.

Rebecca paused at the threshold, taking stock of the situation before making herself known. The two women were on the other side of the room, each gripping one end of a large, plastic platter filled with tiny, cutout sandwiches that, thankfully, were not pink.

Allison's platinum-blond-dyed hair was loose and disheveled, the greater part of it no longer clasped behind her head. Her cheeks were flushed a flustered red and her green eyes held the fire of defiance. She was definitely in mother-knows-best mode.

She tugged on the platter. "Let it go, Jocelyn! I'm not finished with it."

Rebecca's sister, a shorter and much younger version of Allison, whose blond hair had yet to need the help of a colorist, tugged the tray back toward her. "You are too finished, Mother! There is nothing wrong with the amount of sandwiches on this platter."

"You have at least twelve people coming here today, young lady. With you, me and Rebecca, that's a minimum of fifteen. You need to serve enough sandwiches so everyone can take two." Allison yanked at the tray again. "Why don't you ever listen?"

"Because that's stupid! Not everyone will want—"

"Stop! Both of you," Rebecca said, deciding if she didn't halt this now, her kitchen would shortly be decorated with flying mini-sandwiches. "Mom, let go of the tray. Jocelyn's right. She's planned this, so let her do it her way."

"Happy baby shower day!" Jocelyn said, her voice changing to its normal chipper tone. She continued to grip the platter with everything she had. "Did you see the living room?"

"Yes, Rebecca. Did you see the outlandish amount of pink this child used?" Allison pulled the tray toward her. "I told her it was too much, but she refused to listen. As normal."

Wow. Rebecca didn't agree with her mother often. Had the world stopped spinning on its axis when she wasn't paying attention? "I think the living room looks terrific," she said to save her sister's feelings. "But I came in here to ask for your help, Mom. I see you're busy, so…"

"Oh!" Allison let go of the platter, causing Jocelyn to back up several paces in quick succession. "What can I help with?"

Thinking fast, Rebecca said, "The nursery. Can you pop upstairs for a second?"

"Of course I can." Allison tucked a few strands of hair into place before focusing on Jocelyn. "Do what you want with those sandwiches, but I'm telling you there are not enough on that tray. The shower will barely get started and you'll be back here refilling it.".

Jocelyn set the platter on the counter while tossing Rebecca a grateful smile. "It'll be fine. Go help Rebecca, Mom. I have this under control."

"Well, we'll see, won't we?" Allison whisked her petite form to the other side of the kitchen. "Are you coming, Rebecca?"

"Go on up. I'll be there in a minute." Her mother nodded and exited the room. Rebecca waited until she heard Allison's footsteps on the stairs before facing her sister. "Can you please try to get along with her today?"

Jocelyn's eyes—a mirror of their mother's—narrowed. "I *am* trying. She's ridiculous! She wasn't even supposed to come with me this morning. She's a guest! But no, she had to force her way into this like she does everything else."

"She means well. I know she's been more high-strung

lately than normal, but she loves us." Rebecca stepped forward and pulled her sister into a tight hug. Well, as tight as she could with a seven-and-a-half-month-size stomach between them. "I'm having a baby. You're leaving for grad school in the fall. For the first time in forever, Mom and Dad will be completely alone in that house. Give her a break."

Disengaging from the hug, Jocelyn said, "I didn't think of it that way."

"Well, start thinking of it that way. They'll miss you."

Jocelyn exhaled a long, drawn-out sigh. "Fine. I'll add more stupid sandwiches to the platter, but I don't see how that changes anything. You're still having a baby and I'm still moving out of casa à la crazy in a few more months."

"It makes her feel good. Who cares why?"

"She's probably right, anyway." Jocelyn coughed. "Just don't tell her I said that."

"I won't." Rebecca chuckled as she made her way upstairs.

Her family was her salvation. When she shared she was having a baby, they'd supported her instantly. Even her story about using a sperm bank to conceive had been accepted easily enough. Sure, there'd been a fair amount of concern, but that was natural. Being single and pregnant wasn't on most parents' to-be list for their daughters.

Entering the nursery, Rebecca found her mother sitting in the antique rocking chair, her eyes misty and emotional. "Are you okay?"

"Oh, honey. I'm fine. I don't know what got into me." Allison shook her head, as if surprised by her earlier vehemence. "Your sister's all grown-up. I guess I need to accept that."

"You do, but I imagine it isn't easy." Rebecca leaned against the wall to support her aching back. "And I'll need you lots after this little one is born. Six more weeks. I can't believe how fast this pregnancy is flying by."

"I'll be here for you every step of the way," Allison promised. "I can't wait to meet my granddaughter. I only wish…"

"Wish what?"

"I worry, that's all."

"I'm ready for this," Rebecca said with a glance around
the fully furnished and ready-to-go nursery. "You don't need
to worry."

"You tell me that when your daughter is twenty-nine years
old, pregnant and doesn't have a partner to support her." Allison blew out a shaky breath. "I know you believe you'll
never love another man like you loved Jesse, but honey-girl,
you will."

Jesse. Rebecca's heart still pinged at the memory of her
first real love. He'd joined the Army and was killed in what
the media liked to call "friendly" fire. If a person ended up
dead, there was nothing friendly about it. Losing Jesse had
been devastating, and it was because of this loss that Rebecca started writing to men and women who were stationed
overseas.

"My decision to have this baby wasn't about Jesse," Rebecca said quietly, adding another layer of duplicity to her
original lie. "I miss him, but he's been gone a long time."

"You still pine for him. And you haven't dated a man in
years." Allison looked away. "As excited as I am about holding my granddaughter, I wish you'd given yourself a chance
to meet someone else before deciding to become a single
mother."

Rebecca pushed out a sigh. Part of her yearned to come
clean about Seth Foster, the Air Force man she'd been pen
pals with for months before an unexpected leave brought him
to Portland. They'd arranged a meeting, and the heat between
them had been instantaneous. She'd known before she finished her first cup of coffee that they'd end up in bed together.

That weekend, along with one broken condom, resulted

in a positive pregnancy test almost four weeks after Seth returned to duty. Sleeping with a man she'd barely met—their pen-pal correspondence notwithstanding—was a complete aberration for Rebecca. Explaining her uncharacteristic behavior to her family, especially when she didn't plan on seeing Seth again, had seemed impossible. That was when she came up with the sperm bank story.

And she hadn't communicated with Seth since. She'd even changed cell phone providers and accepted a new phone number so he couldn't contact her by telephone.

"I couldn't be more prepared than I already am. I really am okay." And most of the time, she was. Even if she felt horrible for her lie. Even if she continually questioned her decision to hide her pregnancy from Seth. "Seriously, Mom. I can do this."

"You can do anything you set your mind to, but that won't stop me from worrying. Or from wishing you had a partner to support you." Allison glanced around the nursery. "What did you need my help with? Everything looks perfect."

Rebecca's eyes welled with tears. She rubbed her cheeks when they dripped down. Darn pregnancy hormones. "Honestly? I just wanted a few minutes alone with my mother."

"I'm here." Allison stepped over and kissed her on the cheek. "I know you agreed to this shower for your sister, but try to enjoy yourself. You deserve to celebrate your child's life."

"You're right." Rebecca smiled through her tears. "Let's celebrate."

Almost two hours later, Rebecca *was* enjoying herself. True, her living room was stuffed with an assorted mesh of family and friends, but the atmosphere held support, love and a fair amount of hilarity—much of which was due to Jocelyn's creative baby shower games.

They'd started with a round of "Who can suck the fastest?"

where each guest had a baby bottle half-filled with punch and whoever emptied the bottle first won the prize. Rebecca's best friend, Felicia, won, which tickled Rebecca to no end.

Next was a relay race type of game. Guests were put into teams, and each team member had to quickly blow up a balloon, stuff the balloon under their shirt and then pop their balloon. Stuffing *anything* under Rebecca's shirt proved impossible, so her team had lost.

Now, they were in the beginning stages of playing "Pin the Sperm on the Egg," and Rebecca had decided to sit this one out. She'd already successfully matched sperm with egg about seven-and-a-half months ago. In her opinion, that made her the clear winner.

"Okay, ladies. I need you to line up," Jocelyn instructed in a loud voice. "When it's your turn, I'll blindfold you, hand you one of these—" Jocelyn displayed one of the cutout sperms, which elicited another blast of laughter "—and spin you in circles. Whoever gets their sperm closest to the center of the egg wins!"

Everyone except Rebecca formed a line that snaked through the living room and into the dining room. She couldn't see well where she was—and oh, she very much wanted to see her mother holding a giant sperm—so she moved to a chair that gave her an unobstructed view.

When Allison reached the front of the line, Rebecca's lips twitched. Maybe it was juvenile to find this so humorous, but she couldn't help it.

The sudden peal of the doorbell stopped Allison's hand in midmotion. Rebecca struggled to stand since she was closest to the door. "Someone get a picture of my mother, please. It will make a great addition to the baby book."

Jocelyn giggled. "You got it, sis."

"Oh, stop. You're not taking a picture of me like this," Allison said, her tone a good three octaves higher than normal. "My granddaughter will not see me…"

Her mother's indignant voice followed Rebecca to the door. Assuming her visitor was a late-arriving guest, she swung open the door without any hesitation.

The first thing she saw was a set of ridiculously broad shoulders. Next was the firm, hard line of a clean-shaven, angled jaw. Her eyes widened and a tremor of shocked awareness whipped through her, nearly causing her legs to buckle.

No. Oh, God. *No!*

A tiny, barely heard moan escaped from her lips. This was bad. Really, really, bad. This was trouble with a capital T.

Seth Foster. *Here.* And she had nowhere to hide.

Chapter Two

"Hello, Rebecca." Seth, looking far too austere in his dress blues, dipped his head in appraisal. "I would've called, but you ruled out that basic courtesy by changing your number."

Rebecca had been wrong earlier. The world hadn't stopped spinning on its axis then, but it surely had now. Grasping the doorframe, she willed herself to hold it together. She blinked, hoping she was experiencing some type of a weird, hormone-induced hallucination.

If so, he looked *good.* Tall and strong. Fierce and confident. Black hair in a military cut that highlighted the chiseled, almost exotic features of his face. And those eyes. Far too dark to be described as brown, but a smidgen off from being pure black. The color reminded her of strong, rich coffee lightened with the smallest dollop of cream.

"Wh-what are you doing here?" she whispered. "*Why* are you here?"

His intense gaze dropped to her stomach. "I'd say I'm the

one who should be asking the questions. I have several in mind. I hope you're prepared to answer them."

"You need to leave. I'm not prepared for an unexpected visit."

"I'm not leaving, Rebecca." His lips curved at the corners in a grin that didn't meet his eyes. Even so, her knees weakened another fraction. Just as they had the first time he smiled at her. "You owe me a conversation, along with a few explanations."

"This…isn't a good time," she somehow managed to say. "I'm having a…um…a get-together. There are a lot of people here. You really have to go."

Seth narrowed his eyes. "Let me make myself very clear," he said slowly, carefully. "It does not matter how often you ask, I am not moving so much as an inch until we talk."

"You can't show up and expect me to drop everything at your whim." She pushed out the words with the intent of sounding firm and decisive. Unfortunately, her shaking voice didn't lend itself to strength as much as it gave credence to her anxiety.

"Oh, but I do expect that. Given your obvious distress at my presence, it seems clear that I have rights here. Rights that you have chosen to ignore."

He *knew*. She allowed herself ten seconds of panic before she lifted her chin. He *couldn't* know. Okay, her condition was obvious. Nothing she could do about that. But if she stuck with her story, maybe she'd be able to bluff her way out of this. She opened her mouth with every intention of doing so when her mother and sister appeared, crowding in on either side of her.

Great. It seemed their timing was as impeccable as always.

"What's going on?" Jocelyn asked from Rebecca's right side. "Who is this?"

One brow shot up and a dash of genuine amusement sifted

over Seth's appearance. "Yes, Rebecca. I'm as interested in your response as they are. Who am I?"

She gave him the evil eye. "A friend...of sorts. One of the military personnel I write to." Addressing her mother and sister, she said, "He—Seth—didn't have my phone number, so he thought it would be appropriate to stop by and say hi in person. He was about to leave."

"Well, it's nice to meet you, Seth," Jocelyn said curiously. "I'm Jocelyn, Rebecca's sister, and this is our mom, Allison."

Seth stared at Rebecca as if her sister hadn't spoken. "Don't you mean 'used' to write to? The last time I heard from you was about a month after my leave, after the weekend we spent together. Do you remember that weekend, Rebecca?"

She didn't bother trying to speak. What could she say to that, anyway? Of course she remembered that weekend. Every scorching second was engraved in her memory.

"Humor me for a minute, while I ascertain my timing is correct." Seth angled his arms over his chest and leaned against the porch railing, looking for all the world as a man completely at ease. "We saw each other in mid-October. We corresponded as normal until the second week in November, which was when you ceased all contact. Would you say that was accurate?"

Allison gasped from Rebecca's left, probably doing the math.

"I've been a little busy." Hey, why bother pretending there wasn't a giant-size pink elephant hovering between them? "As you can plainly see."

"When is your due date?" He paused for a good fifteen seconds, as if to let the question—the insinuation—settle in. "If I'm right, I'd say you're due in what...about six weeks?"

"You're wrong," she said out of desperation. Her mother tensed beside her. "I'm due in August. The fourteenth. *Ten* weeks from now."

"Really? I heard something different," Seth drawled. "You're sure about that date?"

"I know when I'm due," Rebecca said, keeping her voice level and her gaze steady.

Allison clasped her arm. "Sweetheart, is there a problem here I should know about?"

"We should go inside, Mom," Jocelyn said. "We still have guests here."

"Hold on a minute." Seth's jaw hardened as he looked from Allison to Jocelyn. "Maybe I should be asking you two these questions. Is Rebecca due in August?"

"No," her mother said clearly, if quietly. "She's due in July, but I'm sure she has an excellent reason for saying August. You do, Rebecca, don't you?"

"This doesn't concern us, Mother," Jocelyn hissed. "You have to learn to butt out."

"It's fine, Jocelyn." Rebecca closed her eyes for a brief second and attempted to regain her balance. She wasn't upset with her mother for being honest—no one should have to lie for her—but now she had to decide what to do about it. Could she salvage this? More to the point, *should* she? "My mother is correct. I'm due on July fourteenth."

Anger and disbelief, along with another emotion that Rebecca couldn't identify, washed over Seth. "Six weeks, then, just as I said. Not ten. Why the lie?"

"Because I knew you'd jump to the wrong conclusion and I didn't feel like explaining the personal details of my life." Swallowing heavily, she shrugged. "It seemed simpler and more expedient to fudge the dates a little."

"I don't believe you," Seth said flatly. "Stop with the lying, already. Were you *ever* going to contact me?" A pained expression darkened his face. "I was worried when I didn't hear from you. I even sent my brother here to check on you."

He had. She shouldn't have been surprised by the gesture.

Seth was an honorable man, and she should have anticipated that he'd go out of his way to assure himself of her well-being.

But she had been surprised. Disarmed, too. Enough of both that she nearly wrote Seth about the baby after Jace had left. An impulse she might have followed through with if not for the framed photograph that, at the time, sat next to her monitor. The very same photo she and Jesse had planned on using when they announced their engagement.

As it turned out, they never had the chance to share that information with anyone but their families. The photograph had been used, though, along with many other snapshots of Jesse. At the funeral home, on a table filled with memories of Jesse's life.

Recently, Rebecca had packed away her memorabilia of Jesse. She was having a baby. It was time to focus on the future. Right now, though, she was more concerned with the present.

"I told Jace I was fine," she said to Seth. "You did get that message, didn't you?"

"I got it. But he tuned in to what you *didn't* tell him," Seth said, his voice etched with ice. "You tried to hide your pregnancy, but he noticed the signs. And yesterday, he told me everything. Granted, I would've appreciated being made aware of your condition earlier, but at least someone had the decency to fill me in."

"Rebecca? Who is this young man?" Allison broke in, apparently ready for an explanation. "Is he alluding to what I think—"

"Give me a minute here, Mom. What signs?" Rebecca asked Seth, bringing that day to the forefront of her memory. "We had a cup of coffee, talked and he left."

"You had juice, not coffee. You were wearing what looked like a maternity shirt. The kicker was the bottle of prenatal vitamins in your kitchen." Now, Seth's eyes were filled with steely anger. "How could you keep this from me? I have the right to know about *my child!*"

A choked-sounding sob emerged. She tried to process everything that was happening but failed. What should she do now? Spontaneous decisions were not her strong suit. She needed time to reflect on every possible course of action. But Seth wasn't going to give her that time.

"Look, mister," Jocelyn said, taking the heat for Rebecca. "My sister used a sperm bank to get pregnant. So I don't know what happened between the two of you, but you're upsetting her." Jocelyn pushed herself to the front, shielding Rebecca. "I think you should leave."

"A sperm bank? Is that what you told them, Becca?" Seth leaned over, picked her itty-bitty sister up by the waist and gently moved her to the side. "Or is your sister lying for you?"

"Jocelyn isn't lying." Rebecca folded her arms across her chest in defense of Seth's endless questions. "And yes, that's what I told them."

Every part of him grew still and silent, reminding her of those odd, bleak seconds before a storm blew in. When he spoke, it was with a quiet determination that made her heart pound even more furiously. "Tell them the truth. Before I do it for you."

"What's the truth?" her mother and sister demanded in near-perfect unison.

"Um...well." The baby kicked, as if voicing the same question. Rebecca looked at her mother, then her sister and then at Seth. He wasn't going to give up. He wasn't going to buy into a story she had zero way of proving. He'd likely bring in attorneys and DNA tests and create all sorts of havoc until he learned the truth.

If she continued to deny what he already knew, he might even try to take her child away from her. He might even succeed.

"Tell them," Seth pushed, his tone insistent and hard. "Tell *me*."

"Okay! I—I lied. To you, to my family, to everyone. Is that what you want to hear? This baby is ours," Rebecca admitted in a tremor-filled voice. "And yes, you have the right to know."

Her mother's relieved statement of "Thank you, God" barely registered in Rebecca's numbed brain. Everything in her was focused on Seth. On his response. On what this moment would mean for her and for her child.

But he didn't speak. His reaction was a sharp intake of breath while he continued to stare at her in shock and disbelief. In anger, too, she was sure.

She couldn't blame him for any of those feelings. "I'm... sorry. But—" Tears sprang from her eyes, dripped down her cheeks, but she didn't wipe them away. "I had reasons. I...I should explain. So you'll understand why I made the decision I did."

This wasn't about forgiveness. In truth, it would probably be best if Seth never forgave her. She needed to keep as much distance between them as possible, and if he disliked her, doing so would be a heck of a lot easier.

She had no need for a man in her life. Especially a man who made everything inside of her melt when she so much as glanced in his direction. She'd felt the same for Jesse. Who'd then served their country and left her with a hole in her heart that had yet to completely heal.

Seth Foster was far too much of a risk. A military man through and through, he'd already committed himself to his job and, like Jesse, to their country. Getting too close to him spelled danger and possible heartache. For both her and her daughter.

"I will explain," she said again. "And then we can figure out the rest."

"I'm not interested in explanations." Seth swallowed hard

enough that his Adam's apple jerked in his throat. "My only concern is fixing this."

Shivers of foreboding trailed down Rebecca's spine. "How do you expect us to do that?"

His eyes, now so dark they were pools of black, locked on to hers. In one fluid motion, he dropped to his knees and pulled a small jewelry box out of his pocket.

Allison half squealed, half gasped from her place next to Rebecca.

Jocelyn whispered, "Oh, my God."

Rebecca slouched against her mother, needing the support. "Wh-what are you d-doing?" she stammered. "Because it can't be what I think you're doing."

"It seems that you and I are having a baby." Seth spoke calmly enough, but Rebecca heard the weight of his determination in each and every word. Her apprehension increased. "The appropriate action to this type of dilemma is a wedding."

"A wedding?" Rebecca blinked. "You're ordering me to marry you? Is this a joke?"

"I don't joke about my family." Seth opened the velvet box. The diamond ring sparkled in the afternoon light. "Go pack your bags, Becca. We're driving to Vegas."

This, Rebecca decided, was—at once—the most surreal and ludicrous moment of her life. "Wow. I am in awe of your romantic proposal. But I think I'll have to decline."

"Perhaps," Seth said with the faintest edge of disappointment, "I'd feel more romantic if you'd been honest with me from the start. You chose another path, so this will have to do well enough. I'm sure you can understand."

"What I understand is that you've lost your mind. Get up, Seth." Goose bumps dotted Rebecca's arms and she found it difficult to breathe. "Let me be very clear in this. I am not driving to Vegas with you. I am not marrying you. Not now. Not ever."

"There isn't any point in arguing, Becca." Seth stood and pressed the ring box into her hands. The heat of his touch swept through her, electrifying every cell in her body. "One way or another, we *are* doing this. Tonight."

Seth's heart stuttered in surprised relief when Rebecca's hand squeezed around the ring box. *Nothing* had gone as planned. His goals had been simple: remain calm, extract the truth and once she admitted he was the father, convince her that the only logical action was to marry him.

That plan disintegrated the second she opened the door. Time seemed to stop as her crystalline blue-green eyes widened in shock, as one hand came to rest on her basketball-shaped stomach and the other smoothed her chin-length, strawberry-blond hair.

She looked different than he remembered. The contours of her oval-shaped face were softer, rounder. There were now freckles scattered along her nose, cheeks and forehead. Purplish smudges covered the fragile area beneath her eyes. He fleetingly wondered if she was getting enough sleep or if there was cause for concern. And the square-necked, summery dress she wore—a long, flowing concoction of brown and cream—highlighted not only the impressive swell of her stomach, but her decidedly fuller breasts.

The lithe, petite woman he'd spent the weekend with close to eight months ago was gone, replaced by a swollen, puffed-up version of that same woman. But somehow, and damn if he could explain it, she was radiant. And beautiful in such a refreshing, *real* way that it stole Seth's ability to think, to reason, to behave in an expected manner.

A rush of contradictory emotions took control, overriding all else. How could he be disillusioned and angry by her behavior, yet still want to protect her. Care for her, even?

Unable to comprehend how such opposing factors could

exist at the same time, his carefully thought-out plan fell to the wayside. Instead, he'd reacted with the instinctive, primal urge of a caveman, his only objective to claim what was his.

No. Nothing had gone as planned, but somehow, he'd managed to succeed. He glanced at Rebecca's fingers, which were still wrapped securely around the jewelry box, and the tight, frantic pressure in his chest evaporated. The pumped-up caveman inside went back into hiding.

Seth's sanity returned.

"This is logical, Rebecca." He attempted a smile. Unfortunately, his lips refused to budge from the severe, straight line he'd imposed on them earlier. He settled for nodding toward the house. "So if you'll go get your things, we can be off."

Those gorgeous green-blue eyes of hers narrowed into slits, giving him the impression of a cat about to pounce. That didn't bode well. Tilting her head downward, she looked at the ring he'd purchased that morning. A simple solitaire that had seemed the perfect choice.

"If it doesn't fit, we can have it resized," he offered. "Or if you'd like to exchange it for another ring, that's fine with me. Whatever you want."

She pried the ring out of its box with the tip of her pinkie finger, wrinkled her nose as if the diamond had a rank odor and then tossed the ring into the prickly, thorny rosebushes that framed her front porch. The box quickly followed the same path.

With that, she turned on her heel and escaped into the house, leaving him alone with her sister and mother. Both of whom looked ready to kill first and ask questions later.

Tossing a wary glance toward Allison and Jocelyn, he said, "That...ah...didn't go nearly as well as I'd hoped."

"Brilliant deduction, Sherlock," Jocelyn said, not bothering to hide her sarcasm. "Did you really think she'd run off and marry you because you told her to?"

"Jocelyn, don't," Allison said quietly. "Go inside and take care of your sister. Keep the baby shower going, and it would probably be best if we kept this quiet for the moment."

"My guess is it's too late for that, but I'll do what I can." Jocelyn touched her mother's shoulder lightly. "What are you doing? Rebecca wouldn't want you talking to him."

"I'm going to help this young man find his ring." Allison patted her daughter's hand. "Don't worry, I'll be along shortly."

Jocelyn let out a sigh before trailing in Rebecca's footsteps. Seth peered in after her, hoping to catch sight of Rebecca. No such luck.

He considered following her. Surely, given enough time, he could convince Rebecca to talk with him. Except Allison had said they were in the midst of a baby shower. Baby showers meant female guests. Females who were family members and friends of Rebecca, and therefore, would likely view him as the enemy.

And hell, he'd rather drop down into a pit of poisonous snakes than take his chances with a houseful of protective females.

"I wouldn't go in there," Allison said, as if she'd read his thoughts. "Those women have been forced to sit in a crowded room playing far too many baby shower games without a drop of alcohol to dull their senses. They're high on sugar, low on patience and will view you as the perfect outlet for all of their pent-up energy."

Yeah, poisonous snakes sounded considerably safer. Friendlier, too.

Giving Allison what he hoped was an irresistible grin, he said, "Perhaps you could bring Rebecca to me?"

His smile apparently missed the mark, because after bestowing him with what could only be described as a pitying glance, Allison stepped outside and closed the door firmly behind her. "How well do you know my daughter, Mr....?"

"Foster," he filled in, working hard not to snap. "But please, call me Seth. And seeing as *your* daughter tried to keep me from being a part of *my* child's life, not as well as I thought."

"I have two thoughts on that, one of which I won't share because it isn't my place." Allison moved around him to sit on the top porch step. "The other, however, concerns me."

"And that would be what?" Could he have screwed this up more? Doubtful. As angry as he was with Rebecca, he was equally so with himself. Losing control was unacceptable.

Allison gestured for him to join her. Once he had, she asked, "Are you a good man?"

A blunt question. Even in his current state, he could appreciate that. "A bad man who desired your approval would assure you that he was good and decent. A good man, having nothing to hide, would do the same. So, no matter how I answer, you'll remain unsure."

"True, but that's the case with anything I might ask." Allison folded her hands on her lap. "For the moment, I'll trust your answer. Are you a good man?"

"I don't think people can be so easily defined."

"It's a simple question."

"Not really, but I'll play along." The need to do something coiled tightly in Seth's muscles. This conversation might prove important, but sitting here when Rebecca was *hiding* made it impossible to concentrate. "I love my family, respect my elders. I've never cheated on a woman and I can't imagine ever doing so. I don't kick puppies, kittens or any other small, furry animal. But I'm not a saint. I'm not perfect."

"I see." A faint smile appeared on Allison's lips. "What about your mother?"

"As far as I know, she isn't in the habit of kicking small, furry animals, either."

Allison laughed softly. "That's a relief. I'd hate to think of my grandchild's other grandmother being cruel to small animals."

That brought Seth up short. He hadn't considered what the existence of this child would mean to his family. He hadn't told his parents anything as of yet, because it seemed pertinent to first ascertain that Rebecca's baby was also his baby.

His anger, which had begun to fade, ramped up. Rebecca hadn't only tried to keep his child away from him, but from his entire family. His parents had already lost one grandchild. If Rebecca's deception had been successful, they would've lost this grandchild, as well.

Another layer of pressure came to rest on Seth's shoulders.

"I meant to ask," Allison said, her voice pulling him out of his thoughts, "about your relationship with your mother. How would you define that?"

"Normal, I suppose." A sidelong glance showed Allison arching a brow. With a semi-aggravated sigh, Seth expanded, "My mother is nosy, stubborn and overprotective. Clichéd, perhaps, but she's also the glue that holds my family together. And I couldn't love her more."

"Good answer." Allison pivoted to face him. A myriad of emotions darted over her before she finally said, "You should know that a mother's love for her children is unyielding. As a mother, I will do anything to protect my daughters from pain. *Anything.*"

"Of course you would. My mother would say the same." Heavy frustration pooled and settled in his already twisting stomach. "As would my *father.* I have a right to know my child."

"You probably do," she conceded.

"*Not* probably. Without question, I have the same rights

that Rebecca does." This was getting him nowhere. "Look, I need to talk to Rebecca again. Maybe I didn't handle things so well, but she can't lock me out because of that."

Antsy, he started to stand when Allison grasped his arm. "Listen to me, Seth. I will talk to Rebecca, but for now, I think you should go home."

Like mother like daughter. "I'm not going anywhere."

"*Because* I know my daughter," Allison continued as if he hadn't spoken, "I know she'll need time to process your arrival and the decisions she's made. If you push her even another inch right now, she won't react well."

"I'm not overly concerned about the time she'll need to process anything. Sorry, but—"

"Rebecca is far enough along that undue stress could push her into early labor," Allison said, her voice bloodletting sharp. "Your baby is viable, but small. Why take an unnecessary risk? Give Rebecca some time."

"How much time?" he ground out.

"Oh, I expect a few days should be more than enough."

"And if she decides to disappear on me? She has to know I can't stay in Portland forever." God. Leaving now, even if Allison's argument was valid, seemed unthinkable.

"She won't."

"She might."

Allison stood and shoved her hands into the loose pockets of her skirt. "No, Seth. But if it will make you feel more comfortable, *my* phone number is listed."

"That helps," he begrudgingly admitted. A few days. How hard could that be? He needed to regroup, anyway. Figure out what his next steps were. "I'll leave. But this is only temporary. My child *will* know me."

"If I'm right about you, then I agree." Allison straightened her shoulders and gave him the cat-about-to-pounce look he'd seen from Rebecca. "But if I'm wrong, then I'll stand beside my daughter and fight you every step of the way."

"And I'll fight back." He started toward his car, thankful he always drove the distance between his apartment in Tacoma, Washington and his parents' house. Under normal conditions, the drive took less than three hours. Well worth it to have his own transportation at his disposal.

"Seth?" Allison called after him. "What about your ring?"

Pausing, he pivoted. Gave it some thought and grinned. "Let it be. If I know Rebecca at all, she won't be able to leave a diamond ring in her rosebushes."

Soft laughter met his ears. "I'd say you know her pretty well." Allison lifted her hand in a small wave before slipping inside the white Cape Cod–style home that Rebecca lived in.

In his car, Seth closed his eyes and breathed deeply. He was going to be a father. Rather soon, at that. And he only had six weeks to get everything in order. No. Not even that. He was due back at McChord Air Force Base in three weeks and six days.

He'd have to work fast.

Chapter Three

Rebecca broke her concentration from a client's financial statements to reach into her desk for her bottle of antacids. Heartburn, along with swollen ankles and sleepless nights, seemed to be a constant nowadays—though her recent bout with insomnia likely had as much to do with seeing Seth on Saturday as it did her daughter's nightly bursts of activity.

After chomping down the chalky-tasting tablets, Rebecca rinsed her mouth with a generous swallow from her water bottle. Unease cooled the back of her neck. Today was Tuesday. Three days had passed since her baby shower, and not one sign of Seth. What was he up to? Who was he talking to? And when would he bulldoze into her life again?

Now that the cat was out of the bag, so to speak, Rebecca preferred to get the forthcoming confrontation out of the way sooner rather than later. A long shudder of emotion rippled through her. As her mother, her best friend and even her sister had pointed out once they'd heard all of Rebecca's explanations, not telling Seth about the baby had been a serious error in judgment. Well, she'd known she was playing with fire all along, hadn't she?

Yes.

But what she couldn't seem to get across, no matter what words she'd used, was that she felt as if she had no other choice. Every time she'd considered writing Seth that letter, choking fear would settle in and suffocate her until she couldn't breathe. Her heart would race, her skin would grow clammy and her hands would visibly shake.

Ultimately, she couldn't move beyond her panic to do what was right.

Seth knew the truth now; there was no getting away from that. She had to believe that as long as she didn't attempt to put up any additional roadblocks, he'd be content to be a distant part of their child's life. He had a career that demanded a great deal of his attention and time. A career he loved. Based on their correspondence, a career he had no intention of ever giving up.

All of the same reasons that fueled her fear might also work to her advantage. Yes, she'd worried when faced with Seth's anger that he might try to take her daughter away. In reality, Seth's life made it doubtful that he'd go for full custody. He didn't live in Portland. In all likelihood, his visits would be sporadic and, except for longer leaves here and there, short. Her chances of dealing with him more than four or five times per year seemed extraordinarily low.

Rebecca took another sip of her water, feeling calmer than she had in days. Once she and Seth spoke again, she'd be able to set the remainder of her worries aside. She'd apologize and assure him that she wouldn't stand in his way of being a father. Then, all she'd have to do was let Seth's commitment to his job take him back to the Air Force and away from her.

A low knock sounded on her door. Knowing that a client

would've been announced before being sent to her office, she called out, "Come on in."

Alan Sloop, the managing partner at Anders, Weinstein and Sloop, PC, stepped inside and immediately yanked his vision upward. Rebecca smothered a laugh. Poor Alan's discomfort around her had grown at the same rate as her expanding waistline.

She didn't understand his nervousness, but Alan was a good boss. Scooting herself as close to her desk as she could—to minimize how much belly showed—she nodded toward a chair. "Perfect timing. I was just thinking I could use a break."

Alan settled his spare, bony frame in a chair. "I wanted to talk with you about what your plans are in the coming weeks. Your due date is approaching and the partners thought you might like to make the switch to working half days soon."

"I appreciate the offer." She would love a reduced work schedule—afternoon naps would be pure heaven—but the longer she held on to her entire salary, the better. "However, as we discussed last month, I've decided to maintain my full-time schedule until the baby is born."

"You're an important part of this firm, Rebecca." Alan ran his hand over his receding hairline. "We very much want you to return to us when you're ready."

"I'm planning on returning," Rebecca assured him.

"That's good to hear. I'm sure you know that Mr. Anders is set on retiring next year," Alan said, blinking rapidly behind his round glasses. "After your…er…maternity leave, we'd like to discuss your future with us, including the possibility of partnership."

"Oh." She hadn't expected that. Not yet, anyway. "I would love to discuss the possibility. Becoming partner has always been a goal of mine."

"I thought as much. We'd like to support you as much as

we can, since you aren't...don't have—" Bright red splotches appeared on Alan's cheeks. "If you were to drop to half days for the last month of your pregnancy, we, of course, will continue paying your salary as normal."

Stunned, she gave herself a minute to let her boss's words sink in. She thought about arguing. Being pregnant did not mean she was an invalid, after all. Plenty of women worked full, busy schedules throughout their entire pregnancies. She was capable of doing the same. But the carrot that Alan dangled beckoned to her.

It would be nice to have her afternoons free. She could catch up on lost sleep, finish reading the half-dozen baby books she'd started and complete her preparations for her daughter's arrival. Heck, she hadn't even begun childproofing yet!

"Yes," she said, grabbing for the carrot. "I really appreciate the generosity."

"Good. That's settled." Alan rose to his feet. "Let's get together next week to go over your current workload, so we can decide how to best manage your clients' needs. But what's most important," he said with a little cough, "is that you know your place here is secure."

Her wonky hormones kicked in, so she dipped her head to hide her watery eyes. "I'm sure you know that means a lot to me. Thank you, Alan."

"You're welcome." Alan offered her a brief smile. "I have an appointment to prepare for. You'll let me know if you need anything?"

She nodded in response. Wow. She'd hoped to be considered for partnership someday, but hadn't thought that a possibility for years. A sigh slipped out, followed by a yawn. Rebecca closed her eyes and leaned her head against her chair. Mercy, she was tired.

She might have done the unthinkable and drifted off given

a few more minutes when her telephone beeped. "Rebecca?" the receptionist said through the line. "There's a Jace Foster here. He says he doesn't have an appointment but hopes you'll see him."

That woke Rebecca up in a hurry. "Is he alone?" she asked. "Or is there another…ah…gentleman with him?"

"He's alone," the receptionist confirmed. "Shall I bring him back or would you prefer if I set up an appointment?"

Why would Jace be here without Seth? "I'll see him."

Struggling to quell her sudden queasiness, Rebecca swallowed another mouthful of water. She'd only met Jace that one time, back in January. While she hadn't out-and-out lied to him then, she also hadn't been honest. He was probably here to confront her.

The receptionist knocked on, and then opened, her office door. Jace entered the room, his six-foot-plus frame dwarfing the already small space. Again, Rebecca was taken aback by the man's resemblance to Seth.

He was, maybe, a fraction shorter than Seth, but shared the same eye color, bone structure and broad-shouldered physique as his younger brother. While Seth's black hair was cropped close to his head, Jace wore his in a longer, shaggier style that spoke of a more relaxed, kicked-back way of life. If she didn't know better, she'd think Jace was the younger brother.

"Hey, Rebecca," Jace said without meeting her eyes. He shoved his thumbs into his jean pockets. "I'm guessing you remember me."

"Of course." Gratified that she sounded cool and calm, she gestured toward the chairs flanking her desk. "Please, sit down. I'm curious what brings you here."

He stepped toward the chairs, stopped, glanced between them and the door as if speculating how fast he'd be able to make an escape. "Maybe I should stand. What I have to say won't take long, and...um...you might feel the urge to do bodily harm when I'm finished."

"I already know you told Seth I'm pregnant," she said in the same cool voice as before. "I can't really be angry with you for protecting your brother. Please sit. You'll make me nervous if you continue to lurk."

For a nanosecond, she thought he was going to argue. In the end, he gave a loose-limbed shrug and dropped into one of the chairs. "I should probably get right to the point, but first, I need you to promise that you'll hear me out."

Confused and somewhat alarmed, Rebecca pushed a wayward strand of hair off her cheek. "Go on. I'm listening."

"Well, it's like this." Jace squirmed. "When I guessed you were likely pregnant, and that there was a chance Seth was the father, I made a decision. I wanted to...be kept aware of how you were doing and if you needed anything. I wanted to be there for you in Seth's absence."

"That's nice," she admitted cautiously. "Especially given the circumstances."

"Exactly! I didn't think you'd willingly approach me with a problem, but I had to do something," Jace said with a small cough. "Being a journalist, I have...contacts who help me when I require information. A fee is usually involved."

"A fee?" She added two plus two. "Are you saying what I think you are?"

Jace gripped the arms of his chair. "You have a client by the name of Victor Tosh."

"Victor is a private investigator." Oh, hell no. Yeah, bodily harm sounded pretty dang good at the moment. "You *hired* him to hire me? To do what...report back to you?"

"Well, yes. Because you were important to Seth and that made you important to me. But it isn't as bad as it sounds." Jace spoke so fast, his words blurred into each other. "Vic didn't conduct any background searches and he didn't poke into your private life."

She counted to three. "So what *did* he do?"

"Confirmed you were pregnant once that became obvious. Kept me updated on your well-being, if you seemed healthy— which you always did," Jace explained, still speaking fast. "That was about the extent of it, I swear. But it's important for you to understand—"

"I think you should leave." Anger, hot and fierce, roared in. "Before I let my hormones take control and I throw something at your head."

Naturally, she wouldn't. But he didn't have to know that.

"Not yet." Jace smiled a smile that had probably gotten him out of hot water with plenty of women, plenty of times. Too bad for him that it didn't work on her. "You promised to listen."

Rebecca's gaze landed on her stapler. It was an old-fashioned, metal stapler. Large and heavy. She picked it up, tried to replicate Jace's smile, and said, "Talk fast."

Still reeling from Jace's admission, Rebecca took her time driving home. While she wasn't happy with what had happened, she recognized that some of the fault rested on her shoulders. If not for *her* actions, Jace might not have gone to the extent of hiring a private investigator. Equally important: he was her daughter's uncle.

Unlike Seth, Jace *did* live in Portland. Chances were she'd see him far more often than she'd see Seth. So even though it felt an awful lot like caving, she'd accepted Jace's apology.

Good and steamed, she waited a full hour after Jace left to contact Victor, who *didn't* offer her an apology. That didn't surprise her. The guy was only doing his job. He *sounded* contrite, though, and wanted her to continue on as his accountant. She agreed only after he promised to never, under any circumstance, "spy" on her again.

But that didn't mean she wasn't annoyed by the whole mess.

Within minutes of arriving home, Rebecca changed into a pair of stretchy black maternity pants and an oversize yellow T-shirt. Deciding that a walk was the perfect way to burn off the remnants of her temper *and* get some exercise, she grabbed her sneakers from the closet.

Only to discover that she—a twenty-nine-year-old woman—had lost the ability to tie her own shoes. Or rather, she could no longer reach her shoes when they were where they were supposed to be—on her feet. The realization momentarily stunned her.

Surely, she'd tied these very same shoes less than a week ago, hadn't she?

Unwilling to give up on the idea of her walk, Rebecca crouched down and reached for her right shoe…and immediately lost her balance and toppled to the right.

Great. Pregnancy had turned her into a human Weeble. Except, unlike the toy, she could and would fall if she wasn't careful.

She tried her aerobic step next. Raising it to its highest level, she pressed her bottom against the living-room wall, planted one foot on the step, leaned forward and, once again, nearly fell on her face. Fine, then. She'd go about it a different way.

Rebecca kicked off her sneakers, tied each of them into loose bows, dropped them to the floor and slipped her feet into them. Feeling absolutely victorious, she let herself out of the house into the beautiful afternoon. The still-shining sun warmed her face and the crisp scent of rain lingered in the air, left over from that morning's unexpected downpour.

No way was she ruining the loveliness of the day or her

walk by thinking of the Foster men, their oversize egos or the diamond ring that resided somewhere in her rosebushes.

Though that last one was harder. Every time she left and entered her house, she had to stop herself from searching the prickly bushes. And okay, she probably shouldn't have tossed the ring. Even if Seth's commanding, I'm-in-charge attitude had ticked her off.

But leaving something so valuable in a place where anyone—her mailman, a solicitor, anyone—could find and walk off with it rattled her. It shouldn't. Seth obviously didn't care, so why should she? Yet, for whatever reason, she did.

Rebecca swept a cursory glance over the bush as she descended the front porch stairs. Nothing sparkly jumped out at her, so she continued.

It was a beautiful ring. Simple and elegant, with a traditional princess-cut diamond—not too large, not too small—set in a wide band of shimmering white gold. It was as if Seth had glimpsed into her dreams and chosen the exact right ring for her, which was about as absurd as his proposal. They certainly hadn't chatted about her sense of style during their weekend.

A hot flush stole over her cheeks as she turned right on the sidewalk in front of her house. The memory of the woman she was that weekend continued to stun her.

Maybe it shouldn't. Seth's letters piqued her curiosity about the man behind them almost as soon as they began writing. And Lord, how she'd looked forward to receiving those letters. To answering them. And while she hadn't told him about Jesse, she had shared more personal details of her life than she had with any of the other people she corresponded with.

Doing so had seemed natural.

And when she'd finally spoken with Seth on the phone, her pulse had jumped and her palms had grown sweaty, as if she were sixteen and the high-school quarterback had asked her to prom. The sound of Seth's voice had filled her with elation.

She'd tried to resist the need to meet him, but curiosity and a hunger to see his face won out over practicality. When she walked into the café they'd agreed on, his dark-eyed gaze landed on her and a triple-shot of energy, of intense recognition, turned her stomach on its side.

No, she shouldn't be stunned by the woman she was that weekend. But that didn't mean she had to make sense of it. What happened, happened.

Keeping her pace leisurely, Rebecca headed toward the elementary school that was located three blocks south from her house. Her daughter would attend that school someday. Most days, Rebecca would probably drop her off on her way into work. But every now and then, they might walk hand in hand down the same path Rebecca was now walking.

The tightness in her muscles relaxed as she continued, and within a block, her mind cleared. Her hand came to rest on her stomach and when she crossed the street, her thoughts turned to possible names.

Emily, maybe. She liked Sarah and Hannah, as well. Would Seth want input on their daughter's name? Dumb question. Of course he would. Knowing her luck, he'd favor something obscure and untraditional, like the sometimes odd names celebrities chose for their children.

Her stomach tightened with a Braxton Hicks contraction. Any type of physical exercise tended to bring them on, but her doctor said they were harmless. Rebecca paused, let the contraction pass and then started forward again. She'd only taken a few more steps when a far-too-familiar form fell into stride next to her.

Her heart leaped and blood rushed to her head. *Seth*.

"What are you doing here?" she asked without slowing down, somewhat dazed she hadn't sensed his approach. "As of today, I know you know where I work, so don't give me the excuse that you couldn't call to set up a meeting."

"Actually, I did call," he said in that resonant, severe, *sexy* voice that made her feel like a cat being taunted with a bowlful of cream. "But alas, you'd already left for the day."

"And you decided another surprise visit would somehow be a good idea?"

"It's been several days, Becca. You can't expect me to wait forever."

Breathing in through her nose, she stopped and faced him. Dressed in khakis and a casual, short-sleeved royal blue shirt, he shouldn't have held the same austere, commanding presence that he had on Saturday in his dress blues. But somehow, he did. Her eyes slid down the length of him before embarrassment dragged them back up. "I know what you're doing."

"Do you?" he asked in a humor-drenched voice. "Please fill me in. What am I doing?"

"You're trying to keep me in a perpetual state of...of—" Dang it! What was the word she wanted. Unable to find it or deal with his self-satisfied smirk, she settled for, "Weakness. Strike when the enemy is least prepared, right?"

"I don't consider you my enemy, Rebecca. But yes, surprise is a method often employed to achieve the upper hand in most types of negotiations." Shadows, dark and searching, entered his eyes, his expression. "We both know what Saturday was about. I'd rather not waste additional minutes backtracking over already-covered ground."

"Agreed. As long as you understand I'm not accepting your proposal."

"That would be called backtracking, as you made that quite clear three days ago."

She couldn't decide if he was up to something or simply trying to put her at ease. Raising her chin, she said in a bore-no-room-for-argument tone, "I won't change my mind."

"Understood." Seth reached out to touch her, but pulled back. "You look upset. I've heard that stress can sometimes cause problems during pregnancy. My goal isn't to upset you."

"I'm fine and so is the baby." She swallowed past the lump in her throat. "We're okay."

Relief eased the furrows that etched his brow. He bent slightly at the waist, as if he were a gentleman from a long-ago time and she his lady, and held out his hand. "Shall we continue with your walk then?"

Because the idea of walking side by side with Seth was so very appealing, she pointed to the school a few blocks up. "I'm going there. Then, I'll go home. Why don't you wait on my porch and let me finish my walk in peace. We can talk when I get back."

"I'd rather stay with you."

"I won't be long and you…you can spend the time searching for your ring."

One corner of his mouth quirked in a delicious sort of half smile. "Drives you crazy that I left the ring there, doesn't it?"

"Not crazy. I happen to think it's…senseless."

"It's a valuable ring," Seth said with less concern than he might show for a lost quarter. "Someone could find it…probably resell it for a decent amount. Finders keepers, I guess."

"Exactly. Which is why you should locate the dang ring."

"I find I'm…content knowing the ring is on your property. So, Rebecca," he said, lifting his fingers to flutter gently in her hair. "If you really want to return *your* engagement ring, you'll have to conduct your own search."

Her breath caught at his touch, at the tingles of pleasure that teased and bobbed along her skin so effortlessly. "*Your* ring," she said in a husky whisper. "I never accepted it."

"But you did, sweetheart. I have vivid recall of that moment."

She pulled out of his hold, fast, before she did something

utterly stupid and kissed him. Because yes, that was exactly what her traitorous body craved. *Nothing but hormones.* "I can claim what was in my head far more accurately than you can. And I did not accept your ring."

"Hmm. I suppose we'll have to agree to disagree." Seth captured her hand in his. "Let's finish our walk before it gets dark. Have you eaten dinner yet?"

"Um...no. I thought I'd make dinner later." Without thinking, she matched her stride to Seth's when he took off toward the school. "Sandwiches and fresh fruit. Nothing special, but enough for two. If you're hungry, that is. Since we have to talk, anyway."

Gracious. Now she was *blabbering*.

"That sounds good." Seth's thumb traced an invisible circle on the outside of her hand. "Maybe we can go out for ice cream after."

"Maybe."

Seth continued to absently rub his thumb in that lazy, circular motion. Warmth followed his touch, wherever skin met skin, until she'd have sworn a circle of fire had been branded on her hand. She wasn't supposed to be doing this—holding hands with Seth, taking an evening stroll together and talking about what *their* plans were for the evening.

This was *not* what she wanted.

They reached the sidewalk that ran alongside the school. Nodding toward the benches on the far side of the playground, she said, "Let's stop here for a minute. I'm a little tired."

Seth's hold on her hand tightened. "You're feeling okay, though?"

"Yes, Seth. Nothing's wrong that a few minutes off my feet won't cure."

"We should have turned back sooner," was his gruff response. But he led her to the benches, and once there, waited for her to sit before taking the spot next to her. "Is it normal to tire after a few blocks of walking? Should I be worried?"

"It is normal, and no, you shouldn't worry." Deciding to poke a stick into the cage to see if she could wake the bear, she said, "You don't seem angry with me anymore. Why is that?"

"I've calmed down," he said in a quiet, if terse, timbre. "Remaining angry at something that can't be changed is useless. I'd rather move forward."

"Forward how?" One breath in, another out. "I'm confused by your change in behavior. What's your plan here?"

"I thought we'd finish our walk, have some dinner, engage in a little conversation and maybe go out for ice cream," he said easily. Convincingly. "I thought we'd established that."

"What about tomorrow, or the next day, or the one after that?"

Stretching out his legs, he said, "We'll figure that out tomorrow, and the next day, and the one after that."

Had she ever met such a confusing man? Rebecca didn't think so. Actually, she'd be willing to bet she hadn't, and she *hated* games of chance. "Thanks for clearing that up."

"No problem." Suddenly, he tipped his head to the right while his gaze shifted away from hers. He scooted off the bench, and before her brain could piece together his movements, Seth Foster was, once again, kneeling in front of her.

"No! No way." *Thumpa-thumpa-thumpa* went her heart. "I told you earlier that I am not accepting your proposal. Ever. This isn't the 1800s, or even the 1950s. A woman can remain single *and* have a baby. It happens all the time now." She started to pull herself up, which frankly, wasn't that easy of a task, when Seth's hand grasped her foot.

"Relax, Rebecca. I'm not proposing. Though, it bears saying that your repeated and emphatic refusals are beginning to wear on me." He sighed the sigh of a hurt man. She didn't buy it for a second. "I do have some pride, you know."

Not proposing? "But you're kneeling."

"I am." He tugged at the laces on her left sneaker. "I'm tying your shoe, before you fall and I have to spend the night pacing in the hospital, worrying if you and our baby are okay."

"Oh." She took that in and shrugged in feigned indifference. "Well, then. Go ahead."

"Besides which," he said in an irritatingly cheerful manner, "You'll be proposing to me soon enough. And when you do, Rebecca, I promise you that I *will* say yes."

Chapter Four

Seth plugged the address he'd written down that morning into his GPS and put the car into drive. Mild temperatures, lush greenery and a dynamite view of Mount Hood on a clear day—like today—made Portland in June a beautiful place to be.

He'd loved growing up here. If he'd chosen a different career, he'd likely never have left—though the fact he piloted C-17s kept him relatively close to home, as he was based a few miles outside of Tacoma at McChord AFB. When he wasn't deployed or away on an overseas mission, visiting his family on a somewhat regular basis hadn't proved problematic.

Stopping at a red light, Seth rolled down his window. Air, fresh and clean and vibrant with the city's afternoon energy, filled his lungs. Yes, he loved this city. Even so, chances were good he'd never live here again. He'd known for a good portion of his life that he was built for the Air Force. This surety had less to do with wanting to fly—though that need ran hard and deep in his blood—than it did with what the Air Force represented.

His desire to have an active role in the protection, stability and growth of the United States of America drove him day in and day out. Some would describe his unwavering commitment as a calling, and perhaps they were right. Seth could no sooner walk away from that aspect of his life, of who he was, than he could his own child.

A possible quandary, given his current predicament.

That reason alone made it worthwhile to keep moving forward. He'd screwed up his initial plan of using calm, reasonable logic to convince Rebecca to marry him the second he allowed his anger—justified as it might be—to get the better of him.

As much as he despised the possibility of being a part-time dad, he gave the idea due consideration. Yes, he'd see his kid whenever he came to Portland. Later on, the child could visit him. If given no other choice, he could and would make the setup work. But every cell in his body resisted the notion. He wanted more. His child deserved more.

Perhaps he was being overly idealistic, but he still felt marrying Rebecca made the most sense. His new plan was to show her that he was good father *and* husband material until she reached the same conclusion he had and proposed to him. A long shot for sure, but he had to try.

Seth tightened his grip on the steering wheel when the burn of his earlier anger resurfaced. Eventually, he'd have to make peace with that anger, with what Rebecca tried to do. But not yet. Smarter, for now, to focus on concrete goals. He'd once seen the possibility of a future with Rebecca. It wasn't such a reach to bring that future back into view.

The female, robotic-sounding GPS voice told him to prepare for an upcoming left-hand turn. He did, and as he continued toward his destination, he tried not to feel too optimistic.

It was still early days, and last night technically couldn't be called a victory.

Even so, Seth had spent almost an entire evening with Rebecca without once being asked to leave. His stomach did an unmanly flip-flop when he recalled the sultry-eyed, begging-to-be-kissed look she'd given him. The same look that haunted his memories.

Maybe he could allow himself a minute amount of optimism. Cautious, in-no-way-was-the-war-won optimism. Next time, he might even take her up on that look.

Seth pulled his car into the driveway of a well-kept house in one of Portland's higher-income neighborhoods. The Carmichael family home was a two-story Colonial that boasted symmetrical lines, shuttered windows and a squared-in porch surrounded by pillars. A large willow tree graced the front yard, along with various types of neatly trimmed shrubbery.

Unless he'd completely misconstrued Allison Carmichael's voice when they'd spoken that morning, she hadn't been surprised to hear from him. She'd been relieved. He hoped that was the case. It would make gaining her assistance that much easier.

The bright red-painted door swished open seconds before he raised his fist to knock, but not by Rebecca's mother. Ah, hell. He hadn't considered that the wild-eyed, fit-to-be-tied, acid-tongued sister would be in residence. Based on the tight-lipped scowl currently decorating Jocelyn's face, he guessed she was as unhappy to see him as he her.

He reminded himself that he'd fought much tougher foes than a five-foot, one-hundred-pound, overprotective urchin of a girl. Perhaps this particular urchin caused him greater concern than any mission he'd ever undertaken, but she wasn't going to derail his plans.

"Jocelyn," he said in greeting. "I believe your mother is expecting me."

Flashing green eyes narrowed. Her denim-covered hip jutted to the right as her arms crossed over her purple, pink-and-black tie-dyed tank. "You really are an idiot, aren't you?"

"Your mother *isn't* expecting me?" he asked, deadpan. "I can come back later. When *won't* you be home?"

The barest hint of a grin surfaced. "August."

"What's in August?"

"California. Grad school. Going for my MBA," she said in short, clipped syllables that didn't mask her excitement.

"Yeah? That's great. Stanford?"

She blinked in surprise. "How'd you guess?"

"California. Grad school. MBA," he repeated in the same clipped tone she'd used. "Where else would you be going? Had to be Stanford."

"Wow." An actual smile appeared, complete with dimples. "So, I guess you're not a complete idiot."

"Careful. Your compliments might go to my head."

"From what Rebecca says, your head can't get much larger."

"Is that so? You talk to her recently?"

"This morning." Jocelyn sniffed in either annoyance or humor. Maybe both. "Ordering her to marry you was stupid. Following that moronic move up with informing her that she'll be proposing to you was—"

"Priceless?" he filled in.

"Not the word that comes to mind. Try *dim-witted*."

"Not so dim-witted when it's the truth."

Jocelyn gnawed on her bottom lip. "You really want to marry her?"

"I do." Seth looked over Jocelyn's head, hoping to see Allison. Someone needed to save him before the pixie asked about his feelings for her sister. He couldn't answer that for himself, let alone anyone else. No sign of Allison. Seth sighed and asked, "What are you, the gatekeeper? Does your mom even know I'm here?"

"Yes, actually, I am the gatekeeper. And no, I haven't informed my mother of your arrival." Jocelyn spread her arms wide and flattened her palms against the doorframe, physically barricading his entry. "But I might let you in to talk to her if I like what you have to say."

What was it with the Carmichael women holding him hostage on their front porches? He forced himself to stand tall and schooled his features. "What do you want to know?"

"Why are you so set on marrying my sister?"

Go with the emotional or the practical? Thinking fast, he chose the practical. "Whenever possible, I believe a child deserves a two-parent household. To me, that means marriage."

She made a choking sound. "Oh, come on, Seth. You're really taking that antiquated stance? I expected more."

"Wanting to give my child a normal family life isn't antiquated," he argued. Jocelyn didn't look impressed. "Look, if I didn't think that Rebecca and I were capable of creating a good marriage, I would consider other alternatives."

"And your definition of a good marriage would be...?"

Sweat began to form on the back of his neck. "I'd start with mutual respect, similar goals and the ability for each party to communicate without throwing breakable objects at each other."

Jocelyn arched an eyebrow. "And?"

"Ah...let's see." This girl was tough enough to lead an Army into battle. "A good sense of humor is also important. You know, the best medicine and all that."

"Bravo, Seth." Jocelyn brought her hands together in a few halfhearted claps. "Great answers if my parents ask that question. Geez, add in a bit about love and romance and taking care of Rebecca and even my father will adore you. But right now, it's just you and me."

"I gave you a truthful response." Damn if he didn't feel like he was talking to his commander. What did she want to hear that he hadn't said? "Compromise!" he nearly shouted. "Obviously, a good marriage takes a fair amount of compromise."

"Hmm. Yes." Jocelyn leaned forward and slugged him on his bicep as if they were buddies sharing war stories over a beer. "What about toe-curling sex? I don't know. I'd think hot, crazy, mind-blowing sex would be a vital ingredient in a strong marriage."

Red, itchy heat crawled up Seth's neck. He yanked at his suddenly too-tight collar to relieve the discomfort. "It…ah… wouldn't be a detriment."

The corners of Jocelyn's lips twitched. "So I can safely assume that you and my sister—"

"That's all I'm saying on that topic, kid."

"Chicken?"

"You bet." Especially when it came to discussing sex with Rebecca's baby sister. "You're very scary for a pixie. Anyone ever tell you that before?"

"Constantly. Speaking my mind tends to rattle people into blurting out unseemly bits of fun information. Which is why I do it." She lifted her shoulders in a small shrug. "You hold your own better than most."

"Does that mean I can come in?"

"Well…you and Rebecca *are* having a baby together."

"We are."

Jocelyn wrinkled her nose. "And I suppose Rebecca could do worse."

"Again with the compliments?" Seth teased.

She looked at him long and hard before expelling the most dramatic of sighs. "It pains me to say this, but I might actually like you."

Yeah, well. He sort of liked her, too. "Pace yourself, Jocelyn."

"Come on in," she said, jerking her chin toward the interior of the house. "My mother is waiting for you by the pool, ready and willing to offer advice."

A strange combination of exasperation, amusement and pride struck Seth. Was this what having a sister felt like? Maybe. He tugged on a lock of her hair. "Are you telling me I managed to defeat the mighty gatekeeper?"

"For now. But we're far from done." Jocelyn shimmied to the side so Seth could enter. "Because if you're really serious about marrying Rebecca, you're going to need *my* help."

Wonderful.

Thursday evening, Rebecca waited outside the room where her birthing class was set to start in less than ten minutes. Stuffing the pillow she held under her arm, she glanced at her watch for the umpteenth time. Naturally, Jocelyn would be late. Rebecca should've followed her initial instinct of asking her best friend to be her birthing partner. Felicia was never late.

But Jocelyn had given Rebecca a guilt-trip over how much of her niece's early life she was going to miss while away at Stanford. When faced with that argument, Rebecca couldn't bring herself to say no. Now, she wished she'd been stronger.

The mere *thought* of waltzing into a roomful of happy couples with only her pregnant belly to accompany her brought on a chilling sense of discomfort. Even if there were single expecting moms in the class, they likely had partners who had shown up on time.

She was also unbearably hot, which only added to her misery. The beige mommy-to-be pants and long-sleeved tangerine sweater she wore had seemed a good choice that morning, but now a fine layer of moisture was developing everywhere that fabric covered skin.

"Where are you, Jocelyn?" Rebecca whispered. She'd already tried phoning her sister, only to receive her oh-so-chirpy voice mail. No use trying again.

A late-arriving couple, probably in their mid-thirties, gave her a questioning glance. Terrific. Alone *and* caught talking to herself. Rebecca made a point of looking at her watch.

With a knowing smile, the brunette woman said, "Late, huh? I'm sure he'll be here soon." She tucked her arm through the man's. "I'm Maria. And this is my husband, Ted."

Rebecca introduced herself and nodded toward the door. "I think the class is about to start. You should go in before you miss anything." Frustrated emotion bubbled in her throat. Dang Jocelyn for putting her in this position. "I'll wait here for a few more minutes."

Understanding softened Maria's expression. "You should come in with us."

"Absolutely," Ted said with a wide grin.

"Actually, I'm not—"

"There you are, darling!" The all-too-recognizable voice came from behind. Swiveling, she gasped as Seth, dressed in a black T-shirt and dark green cargo shorts, exited the classroom.

"Really?" she asked, wondering how he managed to talk her sister into this. Had he bribed Jocelyn? Set her up with one of his Air Force buddies? Or simply won her over with his good looks and charm? The latter, probably. "I can't believe you are—"

"Already here?" He gave her a long-lashed wink. "I've been waiting in the room for a while. Were you held up at the office or something?"

"Or something." Rebecca was so going to throttle Jocelyn.

"Isn't that funny!" Maria laughed as she glanced from Rebecca to Seth. "Here she thought you were late, and you were inside this whole time, thinking she was late."

Seth joined in with a deep, rumbling laugh. Maybe she'd

throttle him instead. Really, though, why was she even surprised? "Yes, hilarious," she muttered.

"Well, let's go in, shall we?" Maria tugged on her husband's arm. "Like you said, we don't want to miss anything."

Ted rolled his eyes at Seth in a men-need-to-stick-together sort of way. "Ready for this?"

"Can't wait, as a matter of fact." Seth wrapped his arm around Rebecca's shoulders and squeezed. "Ready, pumpkin?"

Was that a reference to her orange top, the shape of her stomach or both? Now, she wanted to kick him. Except if she tried, she'd likely Weeble-wobble herself right on her behind. Even worse, he'd help her up and make her feel two inches high with his kindness and concern.

She glared at him, tossed mental daggers at him, but kept her voice in the sweet-and-sugary range. "Yes, love-muffin. I'm ready."

"Aw, you guys are so cute!" Maria chattered as they walked into the room. "We hardly ever use terms of endearment anymore. I guess some of that goes away after seven years of washing his socks and folding his underwear."

"And paying for your shoes," Ted said good-naturedly. "Your manicures, facials—"

"Oh, hush. You know I do that to keep myself beautiful for you." Maria rubbed her cheek against her husband's arm. Ted dropped a light kiss on the top of her head.

Their relaxed displays of affection clearly stated their love for each other, even if they no longer used terms of endearment. It also brought about a ridiculous twinge of envy. Rebecca reminded herself that she was a strong, capable woman who'd *chosen* to do this alone.

Anxious, she swallowed and looked around the room. Just as she thought: the majority of the couples sitting on exercise mats appeared to be husband and wife or boyfriend and girlfriend. Well…so what? That didn't change anything in *her* life. Besides, looks could be deceiving. With Seth's arm draped around her, they seemed to be what they weren't.

"Welcome, newcomers!" A tall, lanky woman with straw-colored hair approached them. She pointed toward the back wall. "Grab some mats and find a place to sit. We'll start soon."

Seth dropped his hold, saying, "Why don't you ladies find a spot for us?"

Rebecca's eyes followed Seth as he strode across the room, taking note of the straight way he held himself. To her, his posture alone screamed that he was a military man. She'd be smart not to forget that. She'd be smart not to forget a lot of things.

"Over there." Maria pointed toward an empty space. "There's room for all four of us."

Forming her lips into some semblance of a smile, she followed Maria. Soon, the men were unfolding the mats in front of them. Rebecca eased herself into a sitting position, and Seth—taking a hint from the rest of the couples—sat behind her, cradling her body between his open legs. Her spine straightened in reflex, and a stiff shudder reverberated through her muscles.

Seth's head bent toward her ear. "Relax," he said in a seductive whisper that sent her pulse skyrocketing. "We've been in much more compromising positions than this."

His breath touched her neck and pinpricks of heat gathered, coalesced and spread along her skin like wildfire. Thankful he couldn't see her face, which probably resembled the color of a ripened strawberry, Rebecca turned her mouth toward his. In a silky-soft voice, she said, "Oh, *that?* Until you showed on Saturday, I hadn't given that weekend another thought."

A lie, of course. A bald-faced one, at that.

"My name is Patsy," the straw-haired woman said from the front of the room, "and this is the Preparation for Birth class for first-time parents. Everyone here is in the right place?"

There were a series of nods and a few muffled vocal affirmations.

"Good! Let's start with introductions. Moms, give us your and your partner's names, due dates and anything else you'd like to share." Patsy pivoted and pointed to a couple on the other side of the room. "How about we start with you two?"

One by one, women introduced themselves and their partners—mostly husbands—and shared when they were due. A few stated they were having twins. Gosh. Two babies. If Rebecca were having twins, she might have to give Seth's proposal serious consideration.

As if he'd read her mind, Seth leaned forward. There was a strangled-sounding quality to his voice when he said, "Becca?"

"Only one," she whispered. "Promise."

"Whew," he told her. "I had a moment's panic."

Out of nowhere, she realized Seth didn't know they were having a girl. Her stomach dipped in a quick burst of nausea. Even if it hadn't been her intent, she was still keeping information away from him. That had to stop.

She'd tell him about their daughter tonight. Maybe doing so would naturally push them into a conversation about the future. His one day at a time philosophy wasn't working for her. How could she plan *anything* when she didn't know what he was thinking?

The room grew quiet. Rebecca glanced around and saw pretty much every eye on her. "Oh! My turn. I'm Rebecca and I'm due on July fourteenth. This is..." Huh. *Not* her husband. *Not* her fiancé. *Not* her boyfriend. Old-fashioned embarrassment coated her cheeks with warmth. "This is Seth. The father. We're...friends."

"I proposed to her," Seth offered, rustling the back of her hair with his fingers. "She said no. Even threw the ring in her rosebush."

"Ouch. That's harsh," Ted said.

Someone else laughed, but Rebecca couldn't see who. Her cheeks burned hotter, and she really, really wished she had the nerve to stand up and walk out and leave Seth sitting here.

But she didn't, so she went for humor, saying, "I woke up that day feeling very, very hormonal. What can I say? Some days are like that."

Everyone laughed that time and Rebecca's embarrassment faded.

Patsy clapped her hands. "Now that we know a little about each other, let's get moving."

For the next thirty minutes, Patsy explained the birthing process. Rebecca couldn't concentrate, not with Seth sitting so close. Every now and then, his hand or an arm would brush her back or her hair, and attraction—instantaneous and un-bidden—would zing through her.

It frustrated her, how easily a simple touch ignited her de-sire. Sure, Seth Foster was a handsome, sexy man. But his looks had little if anything to do with her body's response. Otherwise, wouldn't being around his brother cause a simi-lar reaction? She'd think so, seeing how physically alike they were. But Jace didn't affect her in the way Seth did.

Rebecca pressed her lips together and tried to focus on the class. Now, Patsy was describing the early signs of labor. Every now and again, she'd stop and ask if anyone had any questions. Usually, someone did. Seth stayed quiet, but Re-becca continually felt his presence.

Another twenty minutes passed before Patsy moved on to the topic of Braxton Hicks contractions. After a quick expla-nation, she asked, "How many of you have already experi-enced these 'practice' contractions?"

Rebecca raised her hand along with well more than half of the room.

"Good!" Patsy said. "Just remember that these types of contractions shouldn't cause you any concern. They're simply getting your body ready to do the real work when the time comes."

Seth coughed and shifted behind Rebecca. Arching her neck, she saw his hand shoot up in the air. "How will real contractions differ from these pretend ones?" he asked.

Outright apprehension tickled Rebecca's throat. Until that second, she hadn't considered his appearance here as anything but another tactic to put her off guard. Was he planning on being around when she went into labor? If so, would he expect to be in the delivery room?

A startling thought, that.

Patsy smiled. "Great question. But first of all, Braxton Hicks are not 'pretend' contractions. They're very real. They just don't indicate the start of labor. Okay?"

"Got it," Seth said.

"Secondly, for mommies less than thirty-seven weeks, contact your doctor if you have more than four contractions in an hour. Also, labor contractions will increase in intensity and frequency, with an actual pattern that you can time. Braxton Hicks contractions will remain irregular. If you're unsure, drink a full glass of water to rule out dehydration."

A few other raised hands grabbed Patsy's attention. Once she'd answered those questions, she set everyone free for a fifteen-minute break.

When Rebecca returned to the classroom, Seth was standing in place, almost in an at attention stance. The sight of him—the reality of his presence—felt nice. Which was odd and disquieting, and brought about a plethora of confusion.

"Feel better?" he asked with a small, tentative smile.

Refusing to enter into a discussion about her incessant

need-to-pee, Rebecca settled for a quick nod. She lowered herself to sit, and instantly keeled to the side.

Seth reacted quickly, his arms gathering her close before she toppled over. His scent, a rich combination of clean soap and spicy aftershave surrounded her. Without thought, she breathed in deeply, feeding the senseless need that ran through her. His lips came to rest on her forehead, in a soft, barely there kiss.

"Are you okay?" He looked into her eyes for confirmation.

"Yes. I'm not the most graceful of women lately."

"Of course not," he said matter-of-factly. "Your center of gravity is compromised."

"You should have seen me trying to tie my shoes the other day," she admitted. "I had quite the adventure getting the job done."

"I remember." His mouth did that twitchy, half smile thing. "Can you even see your feet?"

"Sure," she said with a grin. "If I lie on my back and stick my legs in the air, I can see them perfectly fine."

Lines crinkled around his eyes when he laughed, and her heart did the *thumpa-thumpa* dance. Seth was a man who should laugh often, as his entire face came to life when he did.

"Well, I think you're beautiful. Whether you can see your feet or not."

Something soft and gushy burst open inside of her. Dangerous, but it felt warm and wonderful, having a man—having *Seth*—declare her as beautiful. Even if she knew differently. Even if he was only being nice. "Thank you. I haven't felt beautiful in a long while."

"I'm happy to remind you," Seth said, his eyes still locked to hers.

Oh. This man was going to be the end of her if she wasn't careful. She sighed in relief when Patsy signaled the break was over by turning on a CD player. The room filled with the sound of quiet rainfall, and once again, Patsy clapped to get everyone's attention.

Rebecca, with Seth's help, retook her position on the mat. Like before, he sat behind her and cradled her with his legs. This time, she didn't stiffen or balk. This time, she allowed herself to lean against him, taking comfort in the rock-hard, strong lines of his body supporting hers.

"We're going to spend the remainder of today's class learning a few relaxation methods," Patsy said. "To begin, I want the moms to lean forward, supporting your tummies with your pillows. Close your eyes, listen to the rain and clear your mind."

Rebecca placed the pillow in front of her and did as Patsy instructed. Seth's legs tightened around her in a physical reminder that he was there.

"Now, partners, massage is an excellent way to relax in the middle of labor," Patsy explained, her voice quiet. "I'd like you to place your right palm on her right shoulder."

Oh, dear. Rebecca had serious doubts that Seth touching her, massaging her, would put her anywhere near a state of relaxation. She tensed when his hand made contact, tried to breathe, tried to think of anything but the full-body massage he'd given her months ago.

"Now, I want you to press down," Patsy said, "and stroke the heel of your palm all the way down to her hip. Then, do the same with your left hand. The goal is to continuously touch, first with one hand, then with the other, in firm, even strokes."

"Don't fight this, Becca," Seth said in a near-whisper as his hand rubbed down her back. "I can feel your muscles bunching up. Just let go."

Uh-huh. Sure. *Just let go.* Easy for him to say, maybe. Not so easy for her. Not when every part of her ached and yearned and darn near melted under Seth's focused attention.

Of course, he would prove to be a star pupil.

"Moms," Patsy continued in the same soft, almost mesmerizing tone. "Breathe in through your nose and out through your mouth in even, slow breaths. Tell your partner if you want more or less pressure. Their job is to help you, so communicate your needs."

Rebecca almost groaned in pleasure as Seth's hands stroked and kneaded her muscles. Her needs? No, she didn't think she should say what her needs were. Not if she wanted to keep the distance she craved. But gracious, this was... glorious. A moan spilled from her lips as his hand traveled a path down her back.

To hell with it. She'd worry about distance later.

Chapter Five

Touching Rebecca had been a delight. How something so straightforward, in a room with numerous other people, could seem so sensuous was beyond Seth. And that sound she made—a throaty, feminine, husky type of gurgle—was enough to bring any man to his knees.

It was fortunate, he decided, that they weren't alone. Otherwise, he might have followed through on the temptation to slide his hands under her sweater, to feel the heat of her skin against his. Would she have let him touch her that way? If she had, where might that moment have led? Well, he knew the answers to that question: regret, recriminations, doubt and mistrust.

So yes, it was a darn good thing they hadn't been alone.

Seth shifted on Rebecca's couch, resisting the urge to pace. After class let out, she'd invited him to her place to talk. He still wasn't interested in hearing her explanation, but he wasn't about to refuse the invitation, either.

Within two minutes of his arrival, she'd excused herself to change into cooler clothes. Apparently, being pregnant was akin to carrying a mini-furnace around with you. He hadn't known that. Two hours spent in a birthing class had made it obvious that his overall knowledge of pregnancy and childbirth fell deeply into the deficient range.

That annoyed him. He disliked being uninformed.

He waited another minute before Rebecca descended the stairs. Besides changing her clothes, she'd pulled her hair into a ponytail. Again, the attraction he always felt in her presence roared to life. Again, he didn't—couldn't—comprehend how everything inside of him could react so strongly to a woman who'd attempted to deceive him.

"You look more comfortable," he said, aiming for easy and charming. "Are you?"

"Much better, thanks." She stepped forward two paces, stopped. "I'd like to talk."

"You mentioned that."

"I assumed you'd also want to clear the air."

"We're having a baby, Becca," he said, sticking with his calm and collected persona. "Seems pretty clear to me."

"Nothing is clear about this." Sliding her hands down her pants, she let out a small breath. "We need to set some ground rules. We need to figure out how this is going to work."

"You're right, but we don't have to do that now. We have plenty of time."

"No, we don't." Frustration simmered, both in her voice and in her expression. "This baby is coming whether we're ready or not, and I'd prefer to be ready. I thought I was. But now you're here and I have to rethink every last detail. You're... Well, you aren't making that easy."

He wasn't making things easy on *her?* The child in him wanted to point out that she was the one who'd put them in this race-to-the-finish-line decision-making process, but he chose to take the higher ground. "What can I do to help?"

"Let's start with how long you're in Portland for."

Not long enough. "I have three-and-a-half weeks left."

Rebecca's mouth drooped into a small frown. "I hadn't realized you'd taken so much time off. I guess I thought you only had another week or so."

"Nope."

She gave a jerky nod and sat down on the love seat. "I made a mistake, Seth. I shouldn't have tried to keep any of this from you, and I hope you can believe me when I say I'm sorry."

He wasn't sure what he believed in that regard. Perhaps she was sorry. Perhaps with hindsight, she'd take a different route if given the same choices today—though it was equally as possible her sorrow resided only in the fact that her duplicity hadn't been successful.

"But neither that nor my pregnancy," she continued in a halting voice, "gives you the right to invade my life whenever you want. That has to stop."

"I take it you're referring to tonight's class? I thought it went rather well."

"The class isn't the issue." Twisting her fingers together, she said, "The problem is that you weren't invited to be there. Just like Saturday. Just like the walk. And just like Jace showing up at my office without an appointment."

"Jace didn't confer with me before paying you a visit, but I'm pleased he did. As to the rest, I can see how my unexpected appearances might bother you, but—"

"Good. I'm glad—"

"*But* I'm fairly sure you'll lock me out of everything if given the chance." Seth angled his body toward her, looking her in the eyes. "I won't let that happen, Becca."

Her lashes fluttered in a sleepy sort of blink that made him want to carry her to bed and tuck her in and curl up next to her. It was an immeasurably compelling vision. One he had to forcibly pull himself out of to focus on the here and now.

"It is no longer my intention to lock you out of anything," she said quietly. "Of course, I understand why you feel that way. Discovering you're going to be a father out of the blue was a shock, especially because I didn't tell you myself. And with how Saturday played out, you're probably emotional and confused, so—"

"I am not emotional," he said flatly, his tone giving no room for argument. "Nor am I confused. I came here on Saturday to get the truth, which I did. Every other action I've taken is to ascertain that you don't forget—again—that I am a part of this."

"I won't. I promise you that."

"Forgive me if I'm not quite ready to believe you."

"Maybe that's because you haven't heard the entire story." Her bottom lip rolled into her mouth, and he was struck with the inexorable longing to kiss her. "If you'd listen, maybe we could get to a better place."

"Why are you so set on explaining?" he countered. "Have you thought about that?"

She lifted her chin. "So you'll understand."

"I won't understand, and frankly, Becca...I don't think you care if I do." He paused, felt the muscle in his cheek jerk and fought to remain steady. "If you're honest, you'll see that this need to explain is more about your feelings than mine."

Her brow creased in confusion. "What? No. That isn't it at all. How can you think that?"

"It's simple human behavior. If I listen and accept your explanation, and then forgive you, you're freed of any left-over guilt you might be feeling. Which is great for you, but what does that do for me? Nothing changes."

"I don't care if you forgive me," she said in a monotone

voice. "But if we're going to move forward in any way at all, you need to know where my head was at."

"I already do. You wanted me out of the picture."

"Yes, but if you'd listen to me, maybe—"

"I'd love to help you out here, I really would. But I can't." He wasn't an idiot. She was right—letting her explain would be the quickest way to move on. But he didn't trust how he'd react. Not yet. "Being angry with you isn't a solution."

"But avoiding the situation is?"

"All I am avoiding is adding another layer of difficulty to our relationship."

"We don't have a relationship!" Her nostrils flared in annoyance. "We never have. We had a few letters and a weekend. Most men would consider that a fling—not a relationship."

"Sorry, sweetheart, but that's where you're wrong. For one, I'm not most men. For two, we had a *lot* of letters. For three, those letters and our weekend meant something to me, and unless you're even better at hiding your feelings than I thought, they meant something to you."

She stared at him without speaking, her mouth clenched tight. Contention hung in the air, thick and oppressive. Unrelenting. On the outside, she was coiled up, icy anger, but her eyes told a different story. There, Seth saw uncertainty and vulnerability. Perhaps even fear.

Of him? The last thing he ever wanted was to scare a woman. Particularly this woman. He let out a cleansing breath and allowed the tension to seep from his muscles. In a warmer tone, he said, "We share a relationship with our child. That connects us. One way or another, we'll be in each other's lives for many years. We're both going to have to make peace with that."

"That doesn't equate to a relationship," she said woodenly. Stubbornly.

"Oh, but it does. Birthdays, holidays, first day of school,

bruised knees and skinned elbows. We're in this together, babe. From here on out." He paused for a second to let his words settle, and then repeated, "Together."

"Not completely. Not even mostly," she argued hotly. "*You* don't have to pee every thirty minutes, deal with constant heartburn or a nonstop achy lower back. *You* won't have to go through hours of pain to bring this baby into the world. I get to do all of that all by myself."

He let her words simmer in his brain for a full minute before saying, "You've sort of lost me here. Are you mad because I'm the man and you're the woman? If so, there isn't a lot I can do about that. Or…is this one of those hormonal conditions you were talking about earlier?"

Whoa. Wrong thing to say by a large margin. At least, that was how Seth took the skin-melting glare she sent his way.

"You didn't just accuse me of being hormonal, did you?"

"No," he said quickly. "I *asked* if you were hormonal."

Blinking rapidly, she inhaled a sharp-sounding breath. "So your explanation for everything I said is based on the possibility that my hormones are out of whack? Really?"

"Well…ah…that seems sensible, based on what you said in class."

"*That* was a joke." She huffed again. If looks could kill, he figured he'd be six feet under by now. "I wish you could walk around for one hour…one measly hour…with a baby planted between your hips while dealing with a full-time job and endless hours of planning heaped on top of endless hours of sleepless worry. Maybe then you'd understand what I'm talking about."

Granted, none of that sounded like a walk in the park. But he wished she could live on his side of the fence for a while. Maybe then, she would understand what *he* was dealing with. Ever since learning he was going to be a father, he'd lived with this sick feeling that she could take his child away from him at any second.

As much as he wanted to say those words, he didn't. Instead, he gave her the often practiced, rarely successful innocent look he used to give his mother when he was a kid and in trouble. "So you're not hormonal?"

"Of course I'm hormonal," she said half under her breath. "I'm *always* hormonal."

"Then...I'm not quite sure what the problem is."

She gave him a withering glance. "*You* are not allowed to say I'm hormonal."

"Lesson learned. I will *never* broach that topic again. But...I still don't know what you were originally getting at. Help me out here."

"I chose Jocelyn to be my birthing partner," Rebecca said, her chin high and her shoulders firm. "You decided—without any regard to my comfort level—to take her place tonight. Now she's missed the first class, and I have to wonder if she'll show for the next. Did you consider how that might affect me?"

No, he hadn't. "You're right. I apologize for not considering your needs in that specific situation. But did you consider that I should be able to meet my child before your sister does?"

"I... No, I didn't." Her shoulders sagged with the admission. "I should have. It's just that I've been making plans all by myself for months. And none of those plans—"

"Included me?" An unexpected bolt of pain hit him hard. Why, exactly, he couldn't say. Any arrangements she might have made prior to Saturday clearly wouldn't involve him. "That was the past. You can't keep me out of the loop. Not anymore."

"I know." Her vision drifted to the side of his. "There...is something I haven't told you. Something you'll want to know."

"I'm listening," he said, instantly concerned. Was there a

medical issue with the baby? With Rebecca? Was she involved with another man? Or... "Tell me. Please."

"The baby is—"

"Is something wrong with—"

"A girl."

"Whatever it is—" Seth stopped and took a breath. "The baby is fine?"

"Yes."

He only had a second of relief before his head started spinning again. "And did you say the baby is a girl?"

"I did," she confirmed. "I hope your heart wasn't set on a son."

"No. I hadn't even thought that far ahead. I mean, yeah, a son would have been cool, but a daughter is good. Real good. I mean, either is good. As long as the baby is—"

"Healthy," Rebecca said, completing his sentence. "And she is."

"Good. That's real good." He tried to imagine a little girl calling him "Daddy," but couldn't. The picture was fuzzy and just out of reach. Even so, the knowledge brought the semiabstract idea of parenthood into true-blue reality. "Wow, Becca."

His gaze lowered to her stomach and he wondered about the baby inside. *His daughter.* Lord, his mother was going to be over the moon at this news.

"I'm sorry I didn't tell you the other night," Rebecca said guardedly. "I didn't purposely keep that information to myself. I sort of forgot in the...shock of the past few days."

"Understood." He swallowed past a thick-feeling glob of something in his throat. "Have you given any thought to names?"

"Some, but I haven't made a decision. Maybe...maybe we can find the perfect name together," she offered, surprising him. Pleasing him, too. "If you'd like."

"I would love to help choose our daughter's name."

"As long as you don't want to name her after a fruit," Rebecca said in all seriousness, watching him with soft eyes and an even softer mouth. "Or a car."

"Deal." Every part of him hungered with the need to touch her, hold her. Kiss her. "See? Including me isn't so hard."

"This is the type of decision I expect to have your input on." Stubbornness entered her gaze and firmed her chin, erasing the illusion of softness. "But I won't let you railroad me into anything I'm uncomfortable with. When I say no, I mean no."

He deciphered the unsaid portion of her declaration easily enough. She was referring to his proposal, to his statement that she would eventually propose to him.

"I get it, Becca. I do," he said, feigning ignorance. "What you said about Jocelyn makes sense, and I probably won't be here for the birth, anyway. If you don't mind, I'd still like to attend some of the classes. Maybe Jocelyn and I could take turns?"

"I wasn't talking about Jocelyn or the—" Rebecca snapped her jaw shut and shook her head. "Wait a minute. If you're not going to be here, why would you want to go to the classes?"

Relieved he managed to alter the direction of her thoughts, he shrugged. "It's important."

"You're serious about this?" At his nod, she sighed. "I suppose I can live with that."

A win. A small one, but a win nonetheless. "Thank you."

"And?"

"Um." Now what? "Thank you a lot?"

"You're welcome. A lot." Sudden amusement filled her expression, lifting the corners of her mouth. "This feels like a negotiation, so shouldn't you offer me something in return?"

He slid himself to the edge of the couch, getting as near to her as he could with the corner of the coffee table between them, and spoke the only words in his head. "How about a kiss?"

She blinked once. Twice. A smudge of rosy pink darkened her rounded cheeks. "That wasn't what I meant," she said, her voice low and warm, and ridiculously appealing.

"What did you mean, then?"

"Just that…" Her blush grew until the tips of her ears were as pink as her cheeks. "Well, maybe you could give me some advance notice before randomly showing up somewhere."

"Sure, if you give me your phone number. I can't contact you without it." Still, he didn't move. She didn't, either. That made him curious. Did she want him to kiss her?

"I'll…ah…give it to you tonight before you leave."

Somewhere in the back of his mind, Seth acknowledged that this was another win. But for the most part, all he could think of was that kiss. And if she wanted to feel their lips pressed together as much as he did. "Becca."

"Seth…I—" The softest, sweetest sigh whispered from her mouth.

He couldn't resist. He didn't even want to. He moved from the couch to sit beside her on the love seat. She shifted to face him, and again he saw the glimmer of vulnerability cascade through her features. And that damn near did him in.

At that moment, he would have done anything—given anything—to offer her whatever security she needed to feel safe. "Come here," he said. "Please."

"I can't kiss you." A nervous treble coated her words. "As you said, we'll be in each other's lives for a long time. Acting on our attraction again would be a mistake. For both of us."

Our attraction. His hope, which had suffered a few blows, revived. "Let me hold you then. Just for a few minutes."

"That probably isn't a good idea, either."

"Why don't we give it a try and see?"

Rather than answering, she brought his hand to her stomach. "Can you feel that? Our daughter is kicking up a storm. Maybe she knows her daddy is here."

"That's impossible—" He jerked when he felt the thumping, rolling, wiggling sensation pushing against his palm. In the snap of a finger, the mood changed and all he could think about was his daughter. "She *can't* know who I am."

"You never know," Rebecca said. "She's been more active than normal all evening."

"Is that the way it is, baby girl? Do you know I'm here?" he said to the belly, feeling like an idiot. But darn if his daughter didn't kick again. Awed and exhilarated, he pressed his hand tighter against Rebecca's shirt. "Wow. Feels like you're practicing karate in there."

Rebecca's gentle laugh met his ears. "That's what I always tell her."

Strong, sudden, *soppy* emotion engulfed Seth. His eyes grew damp and the thick feeling in his throat hardened into cement. Another series of tumbling thumps vibrated beneath his palm. A tear came free and worked its way down his cheek. He looked up, caught Rebecca watching him with the same watery-eyed, gooey expression he likely had.

At another time, he would have been embarrassed by his unmanly show of emotion. In this instance, he didn't care if Rebecca saw him crying. Her hand tightened around his when their baby kicked again, and another blast of emotion assaulted Seth.

The memory of this moment would stay with him for the rest of his life. His determination to marry Rebecca increased to new heights. Without a doubt, he had to find a way to convince her. If simply feeling his baby move brought him to tears, what would it be like to see his daughter, to hold her and then have to get in his car and leave her behind?

Impossible, deplorable and heartbreaking. That was how.

* * *

Rebecca held very still as Seth splayed his hands over the curve of her stomach, seemingly enraptured by the jostling baby inside. A mistake, maybe, in having him touch her. Her goal had been to derail the intimacy, the intensity, of a kiss. As it turned out, kissing Seth might have proved the safer choice.

Their baby wiggled some more, and a myriad of expressions darted over Seth. Rebecca found herself intrigued by every one of them. This man, normally so strong and unrelenting, had turned into a pile of mush right in front of her. Seeing him this way both disarmed and fascinated her. Scared her a little, too.

The connection between them morphed into something more concrete the longer his hands stayed on her stomach. Every instance their eyes met, she saw a piece of herself, of her heart, reflected in his gaze. She hadn't expected that. As supportive as her family and friends were, no one else could truly understand the absolute love she already felt for her daughter.

No one, it seemed, but Seth.

He reminded her of Jesse. In ways far deeper than she'd originally thought. Jesse had also been decisive and focused on anything that mattered to him. He'd grabbed on to life with his entire being, propelling himself from one adventure to the next with barely a breath in between. And yes, if she'd done to Jesse what she'd done to Seth…he'd have reacted similarly.

Though there were differences between the two men, as well. Try as she might, she couldn't see Jesse attending a birthing class if he wasn't going to be present for the birth. She also didn't think he would have become so emotional over feeling his unborn baby move. Oh, he'd have found the first few kicks interesting, but most of his bonding wouldn't have happened until after the baby's birth.

So no, she didn't actually see Jesse when she looked at Seth. But she had to wonder if the universe was playing a joke on her by giving her a man to love, only to yank him out of her arms. And now, by bringing her a man who was enough like Jesse to initially capture her attention, but different enough to raise her curiosity.

Seth made her want and dream and hope in ways that Jesse never had. And as strong as her love had been for Jesse, an intrinsic knowledge told her that she would fall harder for Seth.

If she allowed herself to risk it all again. Naturally, she wouldn't. She would be a very foolish woman to take the same path twice, despite how much that path beckoned.

Grasping Seth's hands with hers, she halted their slow exploration of their daughter's movements. "It's getting late," she said as way of an explanation.

He pulled back. "How do you get anything done? I could spend hours feeling her move."

"I know." Rebecca moved a few inches away, desperate for space. "It never stops being wondrous. She hiccups sometimes. And she kicks a lot when I have music playing."

"What type of music?"

"Any type. She doesn't seem all that particular in her tastes just yet."

Seth brushed his fingers along her arm, causing Rebecca's heart to skip a beat. "Is there anything you need that you don't have? I want to help, Becca."

His touch electrified her. His words warmed her soul. "I don't think so."

Disappointment settled over Seth. "Nothing at all?"

"I…I could use a ride to my next doctor's appointment," she blurted, making the offer without understanding why. "I can never find a parking space close to the office building."

"I can absolutely do that. When?"

"Monday at three. I suppose you could even come to

the appointment with me." What was wrong with her? Her brain ordered her to rescind the suggestion *now,* but her heart wouldn't let her. "In case you have any questions for the doctor."

"That would be great." Curiosity entered his eyes. "What's changed here? Why are you suddenly so accommodating?"

"You said we needed to make peace with each other. That's what I'm doing." He continued to watch her in silence, forcing her to say, "I'm *trying,* okay?"

"All right." He rubbed his hand over his jaw. "Where should I pick you up on Monday?"

"Work. You'll have to return me to my car after, but—"

"Unnecessary," he said in a decisive way that bore no room for argument. "I'll drive you to work and then return to get you for the appointment. What time should I be here?"

"Six in the morning." This man was surely going to drive her crazy. "I think we're done for now, right? Let me write down that phone number...so you can leave."

His forthcoming laugh was low and deep, and made everything inside of her hollow out. He pulled his phone from his pocket, pressed a few keys, and said, "What's the number?"

She rattled it off. "No more excuses for dropping in without calling first."

Another press of a key and the phone disappeared in his pocket again. "I can think of several reasons why I might choose to surprise you."

"Let's go with no on that one." She walked to the front door, ready to be alone and hoping he'd follow. He did. Pulling her courage to the surface, she said, "We don't have to see each other every single day. I'm not going anywhere and the baby isn't here yet. I'm sure you have friends and family to see while you're home."

"I *want* to see you every day. And, as you so eloquently stated, we have a lot to discuss."

"But *you* said we have plenty of time," she argued, now finding it difficult to breathe. *Why* did he get to her on such a bone-deep level? "Several weeks, right?"

"Yup, but that doesn't change how often I want to see you."

"I'm still adjusting, and I know this is my fault," she said hurriedly. "But I can't process this quickly. Maybe…maybe we can get together a couple of times per week?"

Darkness thinned his complexion for a millisecond. "I guess that's fair."

"Thank you. So…we'll see how Monday goes, and we can plan from there?"

"Sure," he said, his attention wholly centered on her.

"Okay. Good." Her temperature raised a degree every second he stared. "So…um…good night. And drive safe."

"You look tired." In less than a second, he was right there, right in front of her. Her breath caught in her chest when he caressed his thumb beneath her eyes. Warmth sank in and trembles teased and danced over her skin. "Get some sleep, sweetheart."

"I will." For a second that seemed an eternity, she thought he might kiss her. This time, she wasn't sure if she had the strength to turn him away.

But he didn't. Just nodded and left. She watched him back out of her driveway. Her fingers touched her lips in recollection of Seth's kisses. They were gentle and sweet one second, intense and scorching the next. Not so different from the man himself.

Rebecca sighed. The next three and a half weeks were sure to be difficult. But soon enough, she'd be a single mother and Seth would return to Tacoma.

Which was exactly what she wanted, right? Right.

Somehow, the thought left her slightly off balance, as if she stood on unsteady ground that was waiting to crack open and swallow her whole. Thinking back, she realized the sen-

sation wasn't entirely new. It had started with Seth's outlandish proposal less than a week ago. Would he have actually
married her if she'd said yes? Probably.

Seth was a man who believed in commitment, and he
wouldn't have asked unless he meant to commit. *To her.*

A slight tilt of her chin drew her vision to the window, to
the rosebushes where Seth's diamond ring remained hidden.
The compulsion to run outside and look for the ring came
over her. Only in order to put it somewhere safe, of course.
She'd be able to stop worrying about it, and Seth wouldn't
have to know, and— But he would.

Somehow, he would absolutely know she'd found *his* ring.
Forget that.

Rebecca closed the door with a resounding smack and
went to the kitchen to prepare dinner. She had many other
amazing topics to think about: her daughter, the possibility
of making partner, her friends and family. Living her life the
way she chose.

So, no. No way was she thinking about Seth *or* searching for his ring.

Chapter Six

The following morning, Seth found his parents in the living room, casually chatting over cups of coffee. John Foster had retired close to a year ago, and Seth knew his dad enjoyed his laid-back mornings. From what he'd heard from his brothers, he also knew his mother had gone through a slight adjustment period in meshing her schedule with her husband's.

Now, though, she appeared as content as his dad. Seth liked seeing his parents happy. Their well-being centered his world and his place in it, regardless of his age or how far away from home he might be. Once his daughter was born, her happiness would affect him even more.

His daughter. What an incredible thought that was. Less than a week ago, life had seemed far less complicated. Emptier, as well, although he hadn't realized that then. And even with his nonstop internal debate over Rebecca's behavior and his conflicting emotions toward her, he wouldn't turn back the clock for anything.

His parents had yet to notice him, so he mulled over his options. Should he tell them about the baby now? Part of him couldn't wait to share the news. The other part had hoped he'd also have a wedding to announce. Unfortunately, he wasn't entirely certain if that would ever happen—let alone, when. So yeah, he supposed now was as good a time as any.

"Morning," he said, entering the room. "Are those blueberry muffins I smell?"

"They are." Karen was on her feet in an instant. "Let me get you a plate."

"Mom, no," Seth said, stopping her before she barreled off to the kitchen. "I can get my own. But I'd like a few minutes to chat with you and Dad first."

"Have you made a decision, then?" Karen swallowed and darted a glance toward her husband. "About what your plans are for September?"

Seth blinked. His ten-year commitment with the Air Force ended in September, and while he thought he knew what his plans were, now wasn't the time for that discussion. "This isn't about that. There's something more important I need to tell you both."

Fine lines on her forehead creased in concern as she sat down. "Are you healthy?"

"Yes," he promised. "Perfectly healthy."

John's bright blue-eyed gaze narrowed. "We've wondered what's been eating at you."

Seth wasn't surprised. When he was younger, he used to think his parents could literally read his mind. He felt a little like that now.

"I'd already decided that we were having this conversation today," Karen said in determination. "If you were around long enough for me to get five minutes with you, that is."

Ouch. Her intent wasn't to scold him, but Seth felt bad nonetheless. After being deployed for so long, the expectation was that he'd spend the majority of his leave with his family. "I'm sorry for that, but it couldn't be helped."

One eyebrow lifted in question. "It's fine. You're a grown man, after all. We've missed you, though." Her warm brown eyes darkened to one shade shy of black in concern and curiosity. "Sit down, honey. Tell us what's on your mind."

Seth situated himself on the small sofa so he could easily see both of his parents. He believed they'd be excited, but what if he was wrong?

"This is harder than I expected, but here goes," Seth said, wishing he'd put more thought into how he was going to break the news. "When I was home in October, I met with a woman I'd been corresponding with via a military pen-pal organization. Her name is Rebecca Carmichael, and she lives here in Portland."

"Oh!" His mother's expressive face lost all traces of apprehension. Joy took over, and dammit, he knew exactly where her thoughts were headed. "So that's where you've been spending so much of your time? With this Rebecca?"

"A lot of it, yes. But Mom, don't get carried away. It isn't quite what you think." Not yet, anyway. "We…ah…spent a weekend together in October, at her place. And…" He trailed off, his tongue feeling three sizes too large for his mouth.

John laughed. "Spit it out, Seth. We're all adults here, and your mother and I aren't under any delusions that you've saved yourself for marriage."

"Right. Of course not." Suddenly hot, Seth swiped his hand over his jaw. Sweat bubbled on the back of his neck, so he wiped that away, too. "All right then, I'll just say it. Rebecca and I, while we used birth control…ah… Well, it turns out that birth control isn't always effective."

A resounding silence encased the room for a solid minute before Karen said, "Goodness, Seth. Is she pregnant? Is that what you're saying?"

"Yes, she's pregnant." He coughed to clear the scratch in his throat and to give him a few seconds to consider how much he should say. As little as possible, he decided. There wasn't any reason for his parents to be upset with Jace or Rebecca. "I would've told you sooner, but I only found out a few days ago. She…ah…wanted to tell me face-to-face."

His mother sat still and quiet, absorbing the news. His father combed his fingers through his hair, nodded slowly and said, "I suppose that makes a certain amount of sense. I can understand why she'd choose to wait, but you must have been shocked by the news."

"It was a shock," Seth admitted. "Every now and again, it still is."

"Also understandable. How are you holding up?"

"Better than before, and I'm excited about becoming a father." Seth shrugged and offered a weak smile. "Somewhat nervous too, I guess. But I haven't known for that long."

"Having a child is a major life change for any person," John said, as easygoing as always, no matter the circumstance. It was a trait that Seth had always appreciated. More so now than ever before. "I'd worry if you weren't nervous."

"A baby. Such a miracle," Karen said in a near whisper. She gripped her coffee cup tightly with both hands and took a fortifying sip. With her equilibrium restored, she leveled her gaze with Seth's. "When is Rebecca due? And when can we meet her?"

"She's due in the middle of July, so about five weeks from now. As to meeting her…I'll have to see what her schedule looks like."

Something in his tone must have hinted at his turmoil, because his mother's back stiffened and the lines in her forehead returned. "I'd think she'd be happy to make time in her schedule to meet your family. Unless… What aren't you telling us, Seth? What is your relationship with Rebecca? Is there a wedding in the works, or...?"

Seth held back a sigh. "Not right now."

"Why not?"

Mentally flipping through and disposing of a dozen possible answers, he grasped onto Rebecca's argument from the evening at the school playground. "It isn't the 1800s, Mom. Women can remain single and have a baby. It...ah...happens all the time now."

"I see," Karen said, when she clearly didn't. "You two aren't in love, I take it?"

Seth sent a pleading look toward his father, silently asking for his assistance. John shrugged and motioned for him to answer his mother's question.

"I care a lot about her." He considered confessing that he had, in fact, proposed to Rebecca. But then he'd also have to admit she'd rejected him. "I'm hoping we get to the point where a marriage makes sense. But for now, the topic isn't under discussion."

Karen huffed out an exasperated breath. "If there are feelings between the two of you, then I would say a marriage already makes a great deal of sense."

"The situation is far more complicated than that," Seth replied. "But—"

"Of course it is! You're bringing a baby into this world." She closed her eyes and Seth would bet a million bucks she was counting to ten to calm herself. "This is your life," she said when she opened her eyes. "So I won't push. That doesn't mean I won't hope, though."

"I'm doing the same. Rebecca just needs some time to come to the same conclusion."

"So *you* want to get married and *she* doesn't?" Karen asked.

"It isn't that cut-and-dried." Why had he opened this can

of worms? "She's a great woman. You'll both like her, I know it. She's just very independent."

Seth winced as soon as the words were said. His mother was going to nail him to the wall for that comment.

Karen sniffed. "A woman can't be independent and married at the same time? I wouldn't mention that to Grady's wife or Jace's fiancée if I were you."

"You're right," Seth said quickly. While he'd only met his soon-to-be sister-in-law once, he knew enough about Melanie to know she'd be less than pleased by his statement. As for Olivia, well, she'd probably smack him upside his head. Which, yeah, he likely deserved.

Trying again, he said, "Other than some letters and that weekend, Rebecca and I are still getting to know each other. So let's focus on the baby right now."

"Sounds sensible," John said. "Marriage is serious business."

"Exactly," Seth said, even though he stood on his mother's side of the argument.

"Bring Rebecca over for a family dinner so she can meet everyone," Karen said firmly. "That will show her how close we are, and what a wonderful father and husband you'll make."

Seth shook his head in mild amusement. The ongoing joke in the family was that the Foster boys got their stubbornness from their mother. This proved it.

"We'll start there," she continued, "and if that doesn't do the trick, I'll figure something else out. Maybe I can take her shopping for baby clothes or out to lunch. Or both. You know, women bond over such things, and I can use that as an opportunity to sing your praises."

Seth dropped a kiss on her soft cheek. "Thanks, Mom. But let me handle Rebecca. She's dealing with a lot right now."

If his mother heard him, she didn't react. Instead, she

mused, "So we have what? A little more than a month until we have a new member in the family? And you return to duty in less than that. That doesn't leave us with much time."

"Doesn't take much time to love a baby," John said. "Leave the rest of it up to Seth, hon. Weren't you telling me the other night how he's all grown-up now?"

"Well, yes, but...oh, John!" Karen's megawatt smile lit up the room. "Two grandbabies are headed our way. This time in a year, we'll be planning first birthdays!"

"A blessing to be sure," John said in a suspiciously thick voice. "I'll look forward to meeting Rebecca and welcoming her to the family." He cast a speculative glance at Seth. "Forgive me for asking again, but are you sure you're doing okay?"

His father always saw beneath the surface. "There are details to work out, but we'll get there," Seth replied with a level of confidence he didn't quite feel. "So yeah, I'm good."

He didn't think his dad fully believed him, but that was to be expected.

"Seth?" Karen asked, drawing his attention to her. "What if I phoned Rebecca to personally invite her for dinner? Would that be okay with you?"

"It's a nice gesture, and thank you, but I don't think that's a great idea just yet. She might feel cornered and pressured, and I really don't want to put her in that place."

"Well, maybe if I—"

Smothering a laugh, Seth tugged on a lock of his mom's newly lightened, almost-but-not-quite blond hair. "I know you mean well, but stop worrying about dinner. Rebecca will be happy to meet everyone." Well, he thought she would. "I'll talk to her soon and set something up."

"Be sure that you do. I'd prefer to meet her before my grandchild is born."

"You will. I promise." Seth couldn't wait any longer. His anticipation of his mother's reaction was too great to be ignored. "But I have something else to tell you, and it's a good thing you're sitting down for this."

"What could you possibly have to tell me now that would require me sitting down?"

"Well, it's like this…" Seth paused for dramatic effect. "Last night, Rebecca shared that we're having a girl. I'm having a daughter, Mom."

Karen blinked several times. Her jaw dropped open, and for possibly the first time in every one of Seth's thirty-two years—that he could recall, anyway—she was speechless. For all of thirty seconds. Tears were sparkling in her eyes when she pulled Seth into a tight hug. "A little girl in the Foster family! I'll be able to buy pink dresses and baby dolls and…"

Seth hugged her back. Again, it hit him hard that Rebecca had almost stolen this moment from him, from his mother and father. He tried to believe that given time, she would have told him about their baby. But damn, he was glad that Jace had seen those prenatal vitamins.

Rebecca hung up the phone and frowned, annoyed with her sister. Jocelyn had apologized for skipping out on the birthing class and had promised to attend the next one, but she'd also gone out of her way to compliment Seth. Every other sentence was about how cool or awesome or funny he was, and how Rebecca should give him a chance.

So yes, Seth had definitely won over her baby sister. And when Rebecca had spoken to her mother, Allison's enthusiasm for Seth reigned as high as Jocelyn's, though she'd used words like *dependable* and *intelligent* and *honest*.

Both women were right. Seth had all of those attributes. He was also infuriatingly stubborn, almost antiquated in some of his beliefs, and…absent for the past few days.

Sighing, Rebecca stared at the phone still clutched in her hand. She hadn't heard from Seth since Thursday night. Not on Friday, Saturday or all day today. Yes, it was her suggestion to halt communication until tomorrow, but she hadn't believed he'd follow through.

But he had. And now she wanted to talk to him. Only to be sure he hadn't changed his mind about picking her up in the morning to drive her to work, and then later, to her doctor's appointment. Or maybe more as a reminder, in case he'd forgotten.

Except there also wasn't a chance on earth that Seth had forgotten, and unless he told her so specifically, he would definitely show up at precisely six o'clock tomorrow morning. So why in heaven's name was she searching for an excuse to call him?

She'd avoided this man for months, and now could barely handle going seventy-two hours without hearing his voice? That would be ridiculous and stupid. Not to mention counterproductive and misleading. And, she admitted to herself with a heavy swallow, completely and irrevocably true. God help her. She missed his voice.

More than that, she missed *him*.

Why? What had changed? Nothing, really. Yet, somehow, it felt as if *everything* had changed. Her fault, she supposed, for letting him feel their baby move. The way he'd reacted— from the expression on his face to the tears in his eyes—had gotten to her.

She wished she could blame her overactive hormones, but she couldn't. Her feelings for Seth Foster had started long before they'd actually met in person.

Annoyed with herself, with her nonsensical and impractical emotions, Rebecca tossed her phone on the counter and marched out of the kitchen. She would *not* miss him. Or yearn for him. Or dream about a future that could never happen.

Right. No missing, yearning or dreaming allowed.

Rather, she'd embark on one of the many items on her to-do

list, keeping Seth and his way-too-sexy voice and his coffee-with-a-dollop-of-cream eyes far away from her thoughts.

Difficult, maybe. But certainly not impossible.

With that goal in mind, she went to her bedroom and reviewed the list. She'd mailed letters to her current pen pals yesterday, so that was out. Hmm. She could finish reading one of her baby books, but she doubted her ability to concentrate on such a passive activity.

Maybe she could address the baby announcement envelopes. Then later, when she was enamored with her newborn, she'd only have to fill in the details of her daughter's birth. And seeing as she hadn't yet written her thank-you cards from the shower, she could tackle both jobs at once. Liking that idea, Rebecca gathered the necessary items and headed downstairs.

She set up at the dining room table. One by one, she flipped through the address book, comparing the names there with those on her thank-you list, adding a check mark to those that appeared on both. A simple task, maybe, but it kept her hands busy and her mind occupied.

Everything was moving along fine—terrific, actually—until a new thought occurred. Each one of these people was important to her. Each one of them cared about her and would be excited to learn of her daughter's birth. What about Seth's family and friends?

Of course there were people in his life who cared about him. People who would also be excited about the birth of *his* daughter. Rebecca's hand froze in place and her fingers gripped the pen tighter. Keeping her pregnancy a secret from Seth was wrong. She'd known that all along. A man deserved to know his child, especially a man like Seth.

But she hadn't once considered how her decision would affect anyone else. Remorse struck hard and fast. Nausea turned her stomach upside down. How many people in Seth's circle would love and cherish their daughter? How many potential relationships had she almost eradicated because of fear? The possibility chilled her straight through.

Seth *should* hate her. He shouldn't even be able to look at her without contempt, but somehow, he did. How did he do that? How could *any* person do that?

More shamed than she'd ever been in her life, Rebecca cradled her head in her arms. Maybe Seth didn't hate her, but in that second, she hated herself. Or, at least, what she had done. Apologizing again wouldn't serve any purpose other than—in Seth's words—relieve her of her own guilt. But she wanted—no, needed—to talk to him.

Lifting her head, she looked at the announcements and the stack of envelopes she'd already addressed. Shouldn't Seth's family and friends also be sent word of their daughter's birth? Well, yes. But would he even think of doing that?

Probably not. She...she could offer to send the announcements for him, as proof that she wasn't planning on locking him out of anything else. A small gesture, perhaps, but one she very much wanted to do. And hey, if she called him now, he could bring his list of names and addresses with him in the morning. *There*. She had a valid reason for phoning him tonight.

And if doing so allowed her to talk to him—to hear his voice before going to bed—well, that was an insignificant outcome considering the bigger picture.

Two minutes later, Rebecca was scrolling through her saved numbers. She'd never questioned her reasoning on why she entered Seth's number into her new cell, but she did so now. Maybe in the back of her mind, she knew she'd need it eventually. Maybe she never really planned on following through with her decision. She'd like to think so.

Finding his name, she hit the send key and reminded herself to breathe.

The phone rang twice before he answered. "Becca? Is everything okay?"

"Seth. Hi!" Ack. Way too loud. Going for a softer tone, she said, "I hope I'm not catching you at a bad time."

"There isn't such a thing," he replied without pause. "I'm here whenever you need me. *However* you need me. All you have to do is say the word."

And there he went again, being sweet and charming when by all rights he should be mean and spiteful. "Thank you. That's very nice of you to say." Ugh. She'd just done an excellent impression of her prim and proper third-grade teacher.

"You sound a little strange," Seth said, obviously noticing her spot-on channeling of Ms. Ingersoll. "Are you all right?"

"I—I'm fine. I should have said that straight off." His genuine concern threw her analytical brain for a loop. She far preferred anything she could add up in a neat, orderly column. Something she definitely couldn't do with Seth. "I'm sorry to bother you, but—"

"You're not bothering me. What can I do for you?"

"I wanted to ask you about baby announcements," she blurted.

"Baby announcements?"

"Um, yes. You know…the cards that parents send out after their baby's birth?"

Seth chuckled. "I'm familiar with the concept, Becca. I'm wondering why you're asking me about them. Did you need me to pick up a box or two? How many do you need?"

"No, no. I have plenty."

"Then…?"

"Something happened tonight."

"Yes?"

"Well, see, I… Something important happened and I wanted to tell you—" *Stop!* her brain ordered. He didn't want explanations or apologies. "Um. Baby announcements. I'm working on mine now, and thought I should do yours, too. Because you have people who will want to know about... um...about our daughter's birth, and it isn't a bother, so I'm happy to do them for you."

The phone line grew quiet for a long enough space of time that Rebecca wondered if they'd somehow lost their connection. But then she heard him draw in a deep, ragged breath.

"Already?" he asked, his voice uneven and gravely. "As in tonight?"

"Yes, already. Yes, tonight. That's why I'm calling you."

"Okay. Right." He mumbled something she couldn't quite catch. "So, you're good and the baby is fine? There aren't any problems or anything that I should be aware of?"

"No, Seth. There aren't any problems you should be aware of." She spoke slowly, enunciating every syllable. His genuine concern, his eagerness to ascertain that she and the baby were okay might confuse her, but it also made her feel special and important. And, yes, even more ashamed by her earlier actions. "I mean, I'm a little tired but we're good."

"Tired. Right. That makes sense. Is there anything you need?"

"I wouldn't mind a pint of chocolate marshmallow ice cream," she teased. "And the names and addresses of those you'd like to send announcements to."

"Ice cream. Names and addresses. Got it." The jangle of keys came through the line. "Wow," he said softly. "This is amazing. Where are you?"

"Home." *What* was amazing? That she'd offered to write his announcements? "All safe and snug," she said brightly.

"You're at home," he repeated in a faraway sounding voice. "Why are you at home? I thought you had an actual doctor, not a midwife."

"I do have a doctor, but I thought about using a midwife."

How had his brain jumped from baby announcements to tomorrow's appointment? "Why does it matter?"

"It doesn't. Never mind. I'll be there in thirty—make that twenty—minutes." With that, he disconnected the call, leaving Rebecca lost in a world of confusion.

Chapter Seven

Thirty minutes later and Seth hadn't yet shown. Rebecca took to pacing the living room with occasional glances out the front window. She'd gone through their conversation a dozen times, trying to deduce the reason for his spur-of-the-moment decision to visit. The best she could figure was that he'd taken her joke about craving ice cream seriously.

A flash of light rolled through the room, casting shadows on her walls. Easing back the curtain, she peered out to see two cars pulling up to the curb. Within seconds, both sets of headlights were extinguished. She didn't recognize either car, but she wasn't concerned. Many of the houses here were broken into apartments, which meant multiple families with multiple cars per residence. It was far more unusual when there weren't any cars parked along the street.

But when a pickup truck parked in line with the others, and no one exited any of the vehicles, a tingle of cautious apprehension appeared. Rebecca almost tripped in her hurry to lock the front door. Another furtive glance outside showed the same three vehicles still parked, except now there was a group of people clustered together on the sidewalk.

Should she open the door and ask if they needed directions? If it were the middle of the afternoon, maybe, but not now. Okay, then. Should she phone the police and tell them there was a group of strangers conversing in front of her house? Well, no. That seemed a bit neurotic.

But she'd feel a heck of a lot better if someone was here with her. Seth. She wanted Seth, and he said he was on his way, so maybe she should hang tight and wait. Except he was already late, so maybe he'd gotten tied-up with his family. Or he could be scouting every grocery store between his house and hers, looking for chocolate marshmallow ice cream.

Of course, he also could have changed his mind about coming over altogether.

She dismissed the idea of phoning him again. In the end, she called her parents. Neither answered, so she left a convoluted message about strange cars and people, and how she was probably overreacting but if they got the message, could they please check in with her.

She'd barely disconnected when another flash of headlights swept through the living room, causing her heart to jump. It was Seth, thank goodness. No longer anxious, Rebecca watched as he stepped from his car and approached the people on the sidewalk.

She saw Seth shake his head. He might have laughed. One of the men—wait a minute, was that Jace?—slugged him on the arm. Rebecca smashed her nose against the glass for a better look. It *was* Jace. Seth hugged someone else, and as a group, everyone aimed for her front door.

Rebecca pushed away from the window and let the curtain drop. Okay, so this must be Seth's family. And he decided he should introduce them, without any warning, at 9:32 on a Sunday night? Well, what else could she expect from Seth?

Rebecca fluffed her hair and yanked her shirt straight. How dare Seth bring his family—or any group of people if they weren't his family—to her house without first informing her? Obviously, he still believed she meant to lock him out, which she supposed she understood. But how could their conversation on Thursday not have gotten through at all?

She had a choice here: react the way he likely expected and embarrass herself in front of his family or surprise *him*. The answer was easy. She'd be pleasant, polite and welcoming. Even if it killed her. She opened the door the second she heard the light rap, and with a bright smile and a toss of her newly fluffed hair, said, "Hi, Seth! This is a wonderful surprise!"

"Becca. I told you I was on my—" Seth shifted the bag he held from one hand to the other. He blinked and his gaze swung from her face to her stomach and then back to her face. His jaw dropped open and he shook his head, as if confused.

"Well, come on in." She moved out of the way so everyone could enter, which they did. Closing the door, she gestured toward the furniture. "Make yourself at home and I'll put together some snacks. I have cookies and lemonade."

No one moved. Almost everyone stared at her. Everyone else stared at Seth.

An older man with snowy white hair coughed. "We might have ourselves a misunderstanding," he said with a smile. "I'm Seth's dad, John. And you must be Rebecca."

"I… Yes. I am."

"Hey, Rebecca," Jace said from her left. He gave her a wink and the same half charming, half mischievous grin from the day in her office. "You look…um…healthy. And maybe kind of surprised to see us all, huh?"

"Maybe a little, but that's fine! I love having visitors."

Jace's lips trembled in an almost laugh. "I'm sure you do."

Then, motioning to the honey-haired, brown-eyed woman beside him, he said, "This is my fiancée, Melanie."

The woman nodded in greeting. Another man stepped forward, and one look identified him as the eldest Foster brother. He had the same angled jaw, dark hair and ridiculous good looks as Seth. Well, Jace, too, but her mind instantly compared any man to Seth.

He held out his hand, saying "I'm Grady. It's a true pleasure to meet you, Rebecca."

At a loss for words, she met his hand with hers and smiled harder. There were simply too many people here, and all of them were standing and staring and fidgeting.

"I... Well, isn't this nice," she managed to say. "It's so nice!"

A pregnant woman with long chestnut hair and sapphire eyes eased herself in front of Grady. "I'm Olivia, Grady's wife. Forgive us for showing up this way. We...were very excited."

"Oh, this is wonderful," Rebecca enthused, hanging on to her composure for dear life. Had Seth mentioned his sister-in-law was pregnant? From the size of Olivia's stomach, Rebecca guessed their due dates weren't too far off from each other. Which meant her daughter would have a cousin close in age. "Nothing to apologize for. Really."

"That's very gracious of you considering how we've barged in," said the older woman standing to John's right. She tossed a questioning glance toward Seth, who seemed to be frozen in place. "And very sweet. I'm Seth's mother, Karen. We *are* sorry for this, but we thought—"

"You're *pregnant*," Seth interjected, his tone somehow accusatory and shocked. As if this came as a huge surprise. As if they hadn't already covered this topic extensively.

"I am," Rebecca said calmly, even though her heart was

racing. "Exactly like the last time you were here. And the time before that, and... Oh, the time before *that*."

"You're *still* pregnant."

"Pregnancy isn't the twenty-four hour flu, Seth." Rebecca kept her voice light, but inside she was seething. What was his game this time? "It isn't a virus that goes away with plenty of liquids and rest. In case you don't know, it actually takes about nine months to grow a baby. So I'm not sure what you were expecting, but—"

"I was expecting to meet our daughter." Seth ran his free hand over his jaw. "Everyone here was expecting to meet our daughter. You told me she was born tonight. You told me she was born here, at home, where you were safe and snug."

"I most certainly did not say our daughter was born tonight! I told you..." She let her words fade while she went over their phone conversation again. His concern. His odd questions. Her vague responses. The way his voice dipped in awe. *Oh, no.*

"That something important had happened," Seth prodded. "That you were writing your birth announcements and thought you could write mine, too. For the people in my life who would want to know about—"

"Our daughter's birth," Rebecca finished his sentence, seeing his side of it and feeling like a complete moron. Seth hadn't brought his family here to make her uncomfortable. They were here to meet the newest member of their family. "Except I'm still pregnant."

"I noticed that." He shoved the bag he held toward her. "I forgot the addresses, but I bought you ice cream. Chocolate marshmallow isn't that easy to find, by the way."

Heat flooded her as she accepted the bag. "Thank you for the ice cream," she said, once again channeling Ms. Ingersoll. "And I'm sorry for making you think...I was only addressing the announcement envelopes, so they'd be ready to go when she *is* born. And…um…I thought while I was at it, I could address yours, too."

Seth stared at her. She stared right back. She saw his mouth twitch and felt hers do the same. The twitching became smiling, which quickly turned into laughing. Seth wrapped his arms around her and kissed the top of her head. In barely a breath, everything was okay.

"I can't wait to share this story with my granddaughter," John said, breaking into the laughter. "I'm sure she'll love to hear how her grandparents, uncles and aunts created a ruckus in their excitement to meet her."

Rebecca's good humor disappeared. Right here, standing all around her, were the people in Seth's life who would love and cherish their daughter. These were the connections she'd almost stolen from her child, from Seth's family. Thank goodness Jace had seen through her charade. Thank goodness she'd been forced into doing what she should have done all along.

"You okay?" Seth asked, his voice soft. "I really didn't mean for everyone to come over all at once. They insisted and…I was too dazed to object."

Karen laughed. "You should have seen his face when he got off the phone, Rebecca. He was in another world. Once I got him to speak, I took it upon myself to call everyone." She stepped forward and offered Rebecca a warm smile. "This is my fault. Not Seth's."

"I'm happy you're all here," Rebecca said, meaning every word. "I know it's not as exciting as meeting a newborn, but I really do have cookies and lemonade." She held up the grocery bag. "And chocolate marshmallow ice cream. Any takers?"

There were. Everyone sat down and Rebecca excused herself to dish out the snacks. Seth followed her to the kitchen, going directly to the sink to splash cold water on his face.

After he dried off, he let out a lungful of air. "I really thought she was here."

"She is here." Rebecca gave Seth a stack of bowls and the ice cream scoop. "Just not in the way I led you to believe. I'm sorry for that. You must be so disappointed."

"I am," Seth said as he scooped ice cream into bowls. "Don't hate me, but I'm also a little relieved. I...ah...don't know how to be a father yet."

"I don't know how to be a mother." Rebecca finished pouring the lemonade and opened the container of chocolate-chip cookies she'd baked earlier that day. "So I understand."

"You're nervous?" Seth asked, sounding astonished. "I thought you had it all together."

If only. "I haven't started childproofing the house, I haven't finished reading even one baby book and I've changed less than a dozen diapers in my entire life. So, no, I'm not nervous. I'm...petrified." She hadn't planned on sharing that with anyone, let alone Seth. But now that it was out in the open, she felt better somehow. "I tell myself that I'll figure it out as I go along."

"You will. *We* will." Seth dropped the ice cream scoop in the sink. Turning toward her, he touched her chin with his fingers. "You're not alone in this, Becca. Not anymore."

"I know. And...I'm beginning to see how our daughter will have a better life because of you, because of your family. Seth, I really am sorry about everything. So sorry. I...would change what I did if I could. You need to know I mean that."

Long, inky lashes dipped in a heavy blink. Every ounce of common sense deserted her. Her plan to keep Seth at a distance vanished into thin air. Standing on her tiptoes, she pushed his head forward until their lips met. The kiss was hesitant at first, as if Seth was waiting for her to mumble an apology and push him away.

But not this time. For reasons she didn't wish to speculate on, she wanted this kiss.

His hands fell to her hips as his mouth pressed against hers. Warmth tumbled through her, inch by inch, until her entire body was awash with a soft, thrumming heat. Need and want and an emotion too large to name tangled together, freeing her long-ignored desire for Seth.

Sliding his hands up her back, a low moan growled from his throat. It was an elemental, hungry sound. One that told her his longing was as high as hers. She reveled in this knowledge. Took power from it, too. Teasing his lips open with her tongue, she deepened the kiss. The taste of him made her stomach flutter and her legs soft and her skin tingle with pleasure, with passion.

She was lost in the pleasure, in the passion, when the kitchen door swung open. Startled, she tried to pull back, but Seth held her tight.

Jace cleared his throat. Twice. And if she wasn't mistaken, it was humor she heard when he said, "Sorry about this, but—"

"Get out," Seth said without letting go of Rebecca. "You're a big boy. You can wait another five minutes for ice cream and cookies."

"Sorry about this," Jace repeated. "But there's a guy with a baseball bat on your front porch, Rebecca. He says he's your father, but Grady won't let him in until you confirm it."

Before Rebecca could make sense of that strange statement, she heard her father's voice, loud and commanding, yell that he was calling the police if his daughter wasn't presented to him in exactly twenty seconds. Oh, hell. *The message*.

The only thought in Rebecca's mind as she raced—well, *waddled*—toward the living room was that this was a story she would never, ever live down.

* * *

If Seth had given thought to the most appropriate way to meet Rebecca's parents, he would have chosen a nice dinner out—with him buying, of course—or perhaps an informal get-together over coffee and dessert.

He certainly wouldn't have chosen to meet her mother at a baby shower for a baby he hadn't known he was having, where she then witnessed what had to be the most absurd proposal of all time. But even that, Seth was forced to admit, was better than being introduced to Mitchell Carmichael while the man was holding a baseball bat.

Seth had, after all, impregnated Mitchell's daughter. And then Rebecca had lied to her entire family about said pregnancy. Which, to Seth's frame of mind, meant that Mitchell was probably wondering what the hell was wrong with Seth. Or what kind of crap Seth had pulled to make his daughter believe she had to lie.

So, no. Not a good scenario. Especially with Seth's entire family in attendance.

Once the introductions were complete and the explanations given, Allison and Jocelyn, who had been waiting in the car, joined the fracas. Over ice cream, cookies and lemonade, the two families attempted to get to know one another.

Seth's and Rebecca's mothers sat in one corner. Grady and Olivia were grouped with Jace and Melanie, talking to Rebecca and Jocelyn. Seth was squashed in between his father and Mitchell. Everyone seemed to be getting along well enough, but all Seth wanted to do was steal Rebecca away and take her someplace where they could be alone.

Feeling Mitchell's gaze on him, Seth decided to go for honesty. "I'd wager that you're thinking of a hundred ways to kill me right about now."

"Don't need a hundred ways, son. If it's the right method, only one is necessary," Mitchell said with a straight face. So straight, Seth couldn't determine if the man was joking or serious. "I suppose a good backup plan never hurts. Tell me, do you have any food allergies?"

"Strawberries," Seth's father offered with a grin. "The boy gets a boatload of hives if he eats even one strawberry. Not quite sure what would happen if he ate a handful."

"Gee, Dad. Thanks," Seth said. "Glad to know you got my back."

John Foster shrugged. "I do have your back, but us dads need to stick together. You'll figure that out for yourself soon enough."

"Well, we'd love to have you over for a barbecue, Seth," Mitchell said, his blue-green eyes as steady and severe as the set of his shoulders. "Allison makes a...killer strawberry shortcake. Best I've ever tasted. You'll have to try it."

"Shame on you, Mitch," Allison said from across the room. She aimed a wink at Seth. "Don't spend a second worrying about my husband. His bark is far worse than his bite."

"I don't know, Mom," Jocelyn's teasing voice entered the fray. "I seem to recall Dad's reaction when Jesse asked for permission to marry Rebecca. He sort of flipped out. Of course, once he understood that they weren't planning to marry until—"

"Jocelyn! Ah...would you like more ice cream?" Rebecca, who had been deep in conversation with Olivia and Melanie, shot a heated glare at her sister. "Or another cookie?"

Blindsided, Seth could only stare at Rebecca. In all of their letters, with everything they'd shared, she hadn't thought to mention she'd almost gotten married? This shouldn't surprise him. She hadn't deemed it necessary to inform him about his baby, either, so why mention she once loved another man so much that she agreed to marry him?

He couldn't react now. Couldn't ask the questions he wanted to ask. Returning his attention to Mitchell, Seth pretended all was right with the world. "I happen to love bar-becues, so I accept your invitation. But how about if I bring dessert? I'm an ace with brownies."

Mitchell straightened his tall, lean form and regarded Seth silently for a few seconds. With a wry shake of his head and the slightest of smiles, he said, "Brownies it is, then. We'll have Allison and Rebecca work out the details."

Ten minutes later, Grady and Olivia said their goodbyes. Seth overheard Olivia and Melanie make plans with Rebecca for some sort of a beauty day at Melanie's mother's salon. That was good. He wanted Rebecca to feel comfortable with his family, and becoming friends with Olivia and Melanie was a great beginning.

But he couldn't get the engagement revelation out of his head. Who was this Jesse she'd said yes to? Where was he now and why hadn't the two gotten married? Well, Seth assumed a wedding hadn't happened, but maybe he was wrong. Maybe they had married. Could Rebecca be divorced? Did she still love this man…this Jesse? Is that why she'd refused Seth's proposal?

His blood grew hot in jealousy and in temper. Images of Rebecca loving another man, choosing another man, crowded his brain. It was enough to give a man a heart attack. He held on to his control with everything he had and barely managed to do so. By the time everyone else took their leave, he was hanging on by the slenderest of threads.

Seth knew Rebecca was probably exhausted. And he knew that this crazy, impromptu gathering of their families was as much his fault as hers. The honorable action would be to leave so she could get some rest. The sensible action would be to wait, to see if she chose to come to him on her own, to give him some necessary distance to chill out.

But damn if he could walk out that door without his questions being answered.

"Tell me about Jesse," Seth demanded within seconds of their being alone. "And I'd like to know why you never bothered mentioning him or your engagement before."

"I don't care to talk about Jesse." Rebecca lifted her chin in that stubborn way of hers. "Not now. Maybe not ever. Besides, you had your chance to hear everything and you rejected it."

"What chance? As far as I can recall, you've never said word one about a man you loved enough to spend the rest of your life with."

Her chin raised another mulish inch. "You told me clear as day that any explanation I gave you was about relieving my guilt. Jesse was—is—a part of that explanation."

"You didn't tell me you were pregnant because of another guy? *That's* what you wanted to explain? What does Jesse—" Seth's heart rammed into his throat as the unthinkable occurred. He stumbled backward, collapsing on a chair. "Were you uncertain who the father was?"

"Never."

"Then explain this to me."

"You said you didn't want any explanations! At one mention of a man from my past, you do?" Rebecca huffed out a breath and sat down on the sofa. "And they say women can't make up their minds."

"Not just any man. A man you were engaged to. And if he had anything to do with your attempt at keeping my daughter away from me, then I have the right to know." Seth vaulted to a stand and paced the length of the floor, trying to calm the storm inside. "Are you two dating again? Does he want to raise *my* child?"

"Stop! Please stop." Rebecca's eyes took on the watery sheen of unshed tears and her voice bobbed with emotion. "Jesse doesn't want anything."

"Everybody wants something, Becca."

She covered her face with her hands. "Not Jesse."

"How has Jesse impacted your decision not to tell me about our baby?"

"You're in the Air Force," she said, her voice muffled. "And I don't see that changing."

"I am in the Air Force," Seth confirmed, confused and wary. "And no, I don't see that changing, either. But what does that have—"

"Jesse was in the Army."

"Why is that information important to this conversation?"

Rebecca curled her arms around her stomach and lifted her gaze to his. Sadness and fear lurked in the depths of her eyes, along with a yearning so profound that Seth's heart ached. A tear slid down her cheek, and then another.

And that made him feel like the schoolyard bully who'd stolen some poor kid's lollipop. Hating that his questions, his attitude, had upset her so, he stepped forward to comfort her. But she held up a hand, stopping him.

"Jesse joined the Army directly out of college," she said quietly, tearfully. "He was so committed, so sure that was where he was supposed to be. I supported him. I...I even urged him to go. When he came home after basic training and proposed, I said yes. I loved him, Seth. I loved him so much that I couldn't imagine my world without him in it."

An invisible fist slammed into Seth's gut. In that second, he believed she'd never love him, would never agree to marry him. She loved Jesse. And that was the reason for every decision she'd made. What other explanation could there be?

"Then why aren't you happily married to Jesse with two-point-five kids and a dog?"

Rebecca's face crumpled and tears poured down her cheeks in fat, never-ending rivulets that tore into Seth as if it were his grief. As if he were somehow taking on her pain for himself. And dammit, if he had that power, he would do that for her.

She jerked open her mouth, but nothing—not even the

sound of her sobs—came out. With heavy, tear-soaked blinks she fought for words but seemed unable to find them. This was ridiculous. Nothing was worth this type of misery. Seth went to her, pulled her to him and held her as tight as he could without crushing her.

"It's okay, baby. It's fine. I don't need to know this," he whispered while rubbing her back in long, firm strokes. "I will never bring this topic up again. I promise. Just please, please stop crying. You're killing me here, sweetheart."

Rebecca pushed her head into his chest and sobbed so hard that her shoulders shook and her body trembled. Her fingers grasped on to his arms, digging in, as if she were drowning and he was her life preserver. But the sobs kept on coming.

Seth's bag of tricks was sadly lacking in the how-to-help-a-crying-woman department, and the only things he knew to do were the things he was already doing. He continued to hold her. He kept murmuring that everything was okay. That she was okay, and that he was right here with her for as long as she wanted him.

But he felt useless and scared. Crying with such strength, such ferocity, for so long couldn't be good for Rebecca, for their baby.

Desperate, Seth started whispering bits of silliness in her ear. Anything that popped into his head was fair game. Most of what he said were obscure little facts he'd somehow learned over the years. Not a lick of it held any true importance, but slowly and surely, Rebecca's body quieted and her sobs lessened.

Still, he held her tight. He'd be content to hold her all night and into tomorrow if she needed him to, if she'd allow it. The truth of the matter was he'd be content to sit right here and hold her for weeks, months…years, if doing so were possible.

But he wanted her happy and calm. He wanted her smiling and laughing. But more than anything else, he wanted her to be those things with him. The real truth he'd been avoiding crashed in. Yes, he wanted to marry Rebecca. Yes, he wanted his daughter to know him. And yes, he wanted the three of them to be a family.

At the bottom of all of those wants, or perhaps entwined with them, was the fact that he loved Rebecca. Intensely. Passionately. With all of his heart. He'd known his feelings when he returned to duty in October, but hadn't been prepared to confront them. He'd known he loved her when she stopped corresponding, but figured they didn't have a future, so tried to forget. And yeah, he'd known the second she opened her door eight days ago.

Admitting to himself that he loved a woman who would try to keep his child from him had seemed crazy and impossible. But now, with that same woman curled up in his arms, with her tears on his shirt, he couldn't deny what was true any longer. A weight lifted, freeing him to do what he couldn't do—what he couldn't say—before.

"I forgive you," he said softly, quietly, unsure if she was even awake, but needing to say what was in his heart. "I forgive you, Rebecca. And...and I need you to know that I—"

"Jesse is dead," Rebecca said into Seth's chest. "He was killed by friendly fire during his first tour. We were barely engaged and he was gone. That's why I haven't talked about him."

"Oh, baby. I'm so sorry." Again, Seth wished for the power to absorb Rebecca's pain. "I can't imagine how horrible that was for you."

Sliding out of his arms, she dried her swollen eyes and wiped her tear-slicked cheeks. "Thank you," she said in her prim and proper way. "But I don't think you understand."

"I understand you lost someone you loved."

"Yes...but Jesse loved his job. He was committed to his

job." Rebecca took in one deep breath, and then another. "And he died doing his job."

"I wish that hadn't happened. I wish I could somehow change this for you." Seth captured Rebecca's hand in his and considered what he should say. Jesse had chosen to serve his country, knowing the risks going in. Seth had made that same choice. But he didn't think Rebecca needed to hear any of that in this moment. "Do you want to talk about what happened to Jesse, or how you feel about it, or…?"

"I don't think you understand," Rebecca repeated, her voice thick and unsteady. "I loved Jesse. He was the man I planned on spending the rest of my life with."

"I see." Seth fought to read between her words, because she was right—he was missing something. "Are you trying to say that you still feel committed to Jesse?"

"No."

"Then?"

"Jesse was in the Army. Jesse *died* while in the Army. And you're—"

"In the Air Force," Seth said as full comprehension hit. "So you think—"

"You're too much of a risk. For me and for our daughter. Next time—" she gulped for air "—you go away, you might not come back. You might leave and *never* come back."

"So you thought it better that my child never know me, that I never know her?" He spoke slowly, trying to put himself in Rebecca's shoes. "In order to protect her?"

Rebecca pulled her hand free. "Not only her, but me, too. Don't you see, Seth? I *could* love you, if I let myself. Our daughter *will* love you. And what happens when you…when something happens to you? I can't go through that loss again. And I'm sorry, but yes, I wanted to protect our daughter from the pain of knowing and loving her father, and then losing him."

"*If* something happens to me, not when. And most of what I do isn't—"

"You're right. Of course, you're right. But I don't want to gamble on an if."

"I could also trip and bang my head. Or become ill. Or a dozen other possibilities. You could, as well," Seth pointed out, hoping she'd see what he was getting at. "Waking up in the morning and leaving your house is a risk."

"Yes, but none of that is the same as purposely putting yourself in the path of danger." Rebecca averted her gaze. "I can't keep our daughter away from you or your family. She's tied to you in a way that can't be changed, and I was wrong to...to ignore that connection."

"I'm glad you've reached that conclusion, but sweetheart, my job—"

"But I can't fall for you." Rebecca faced him, her beautiful eyes filling with fresh tears. "Life is about learning from our mistakes, and I can't make the same mistake twice. I...I won't."

There were a dozen valid arguments on Seth's tongue, begging to be said. But he had a feeling Rebecca wouldn't really hear his words, or the truth behind them, in this particular moment. She was tired and upset. She needed to rest. Her health was his priority.

The rest would be there to deal with another day.

He whispered a kiss across Rebecca's forehead. "You must be ready for bed."

"You don't want to argue with me?"

"There isn't anything to argue about. You've explained your feelings and I understand them." As he spoke, he tucked one arm under her legs and braced the other behind her back. "To my mind, our next course of action should be getting some sleep."

Relief eased the tightness of her expression. "I think that's a good idea." He stood, picking her up with him. Her body tensed even as she wrapped her arms around his neck. "What are you doing? I'm not...I don't think we should..."

"Shh," he murmured. "I'm taking you upstairs. Then, I'm getting you some water. Once I know you're settled, I'll lock up and leave."

She nodded and cradled her head on his shoulder, apparently too tired to put up a fuss. Tightening his hold, Seth climbed the stairs slowly so he wouldn't jar her. The warmth of her body pressed against his, the softness of her hair brushing his jaw, and the sound of her breathing raised every one of his protective instincts.

The rightness of the moment didn't escape him. He was supposed to be with this woman. Of that, he was sure. But he was also supposed to return to McChord AFB, to his duty, in two and a half weeks. That also felt right. Of that, he was also sure. Both seemed as essential as air for his existence. Was he going to have to choose? *Maybe.*

In Rebecca's bedroom, he set her down carefully on the bed. She gave him a sleepy sort of smile that turned him inside out.

"Thank you for taking care of me. I'd say you went above and beyond tonight."

"I'll always take care of you. If you'll let me." Her face paled and he wanted to kick himself. "Because... Well, you're the mother of my baby. Your well-being is essential to her well-being. So...um...I'll just get that water for you."

He took his time to give her the necessary time to change and ready herself for bed. When he returned, Rebecca's eyelids were drooping and her entire body radiated exhaustion. Sitting next to her, he offered her the glass.

Their gazes met and held while she drank. The want to crawl in next to her and fall asleep with her in his arms came on strong. Naturally, he ignored the want.

"Get some rest, sweetheart." Seth put the half-empty glass on her bedside table. "Do you need anything else before I head out?"

She shook her head no and slid deeper into the bed coverings. Her eyes closed. He waited a beat before standing. As he let himself out of her room, she whispered, "I wanted to hear your voice tonight. I missed your voice. I…missed you."

"I missed you, too." He paused, hoping she'd say more, but she didn't. The soft, even sound of her breathing clued him in that she'd fallen asleep. Turning off the overhead light, he closed the door. And stood there for a full minute listening, waiting…protecting what was his.

Downstairs, he cleaned up the dishes, wiped off the counters and started the dishwasher. He fiddled with her magazines and throw pillows until everything looked the way she liked it. By then, it was nearly two in the morning, and he decided that returning to his parents' house was senseless. Why leave when he'd have to be back here by six to drive Rebecca to work?

Pleased with the idea, in the logic of staying, he locked the front door, kicked off his shoes and stretched out on the sofa. Sleep didn't come easily, but being here, being close to Rebecca felt right. Almost like…home.

He supposed he'd have to give that some thought, as well.

Chapter Eight

Rebecca woke with the glare of brilliant sunlight beaming on her face. Yawning, she carefully rolled to her side and stretched her legs, readying herself for the monumental task of standing up. It would hurt at first, as the full weight of the baby pushed down on her hips. Her body would adjust, she knew, and the twinge of pain would disappear soon enough.

But heavens, she hated each morning's initial impact.

She swung her legs to the side of the bed, inhaled deeply and stood. There it was; that sudden, pulsating ache that flared from her hips to the small of her back to the tops of her thighs. Silently counting to ten, she waited for the worst of it to fade.

Once it had, she chose her work clothes for the day: a maternity knee-length black skirt, white button-down blouse and a black jacket that mimicked her before-pregnancy attire. She put the clothes on the bed, stopping to squint at the overly bright sunlight dappling across the floor. Too bright for six in the morning. And...she'd awakened on her own.

Why hadn't her alarm gone off? *Oh.* With the late hour and the emotional conversation—confrontation?—with Seth, she'd forgotten to set it. She never forgot and she never woke up late.

"Crap, crap, crap," she muttered, twisting her neck to see the clock. *Ten-thirty?* How was that possible? She hadn't slept that many straight hours in months. And she apparently slept deeply enough to miss Seth knocking on her door when he came to pick her up.

Unless he hadn't bothered to show. A definite possibility considering her inappropriate behavior and the over-the-top display of her emotional breakdown.

Stop, she told herself. She didn't have time to stress over Seth.

Rebecca looked at the clock again. She looked at her work clothes. She thought about rushing through her shower, drying and styling her hair, applying cosmetics, fighting with her stupid maternity pantyhose, getting dressed and driving to work. She considered the work waiting for her, the meeting she was supposed to have with Alan after lunch, and...

It was such a beautiful day outside. How nice would it be to grab one of her baby books and sit on her back porch with her feet up? Maybe even think about what happened with Seth. Maybe even think about what she *felt* for Seth.

But she *should* go to work. People were counting on her and she needed to continue impressing the partners. Not going would be wrong and lazy and could possibly hurt her in the long run. Responsible adults didn't play hooky. They...they...

"Screw it," she said in a loud and clear voice. "For once, I choose lazy."

Before she could talk herself out of her decision, she phoned the office and tried to come up with a plausible lie. No, she'd be honest. Hadn't Alan just about ordered her to take time off?

Five minutes later, Rebecca hung up the phone in a state of shocked confusion. *Seth* had already called her office to tell them she wouldn't be in. She sat on the edge of the bed, on top of her perfectly pressed skirt, and considered how she felt about that.

Probably, she should be ticked. She had a future at this firm, and Seth took it upon himself to make a decision he had no right to make. It wasn't anger heating her blood, it was...

"Your daddy decided we should have a day off," she said as her daughter landed a series of solid kicks somewhere in the region of Rebecca's rib cage. Smiling, she rubbed the moving mountain that was now her stomach. "What do you think, kiddo? Should I be happy?"

She received a pelvic head-butt, almost painful in its accuracy, as a response.

"I'm taking that as a yes," Rebecca decided. "Because I refuse to waste a free day by being upset. We'll *relax* until our appointment this afternoon. How does that sound?"

Within thirty minutes, a freshly showered and barefoot Rebecca descended the stairs. She hadn't bothered drying her hair, and she wasn't wearing one speck of makeup. Heck, she'd considered leaving her bra off...but in her current state, that seemed a little too free for her comfort level. A fact that relieved her greatly when she entered the kitchen and found Seth.

He stood at the stove with his back toward her, stirring something with a wooden spoon, and whistling a tune she didn't recognize. Yesterday's clothes—blue jeans and an untucked, wrinkled shirt—and bare feet told her that he'd stayed the night. Probably, she should be bothered by that. But gracious, the man looked good standing in her kitchen.

So she stayed put and sniffed the air experimentally. Cinnamon and spice. A pitcher of orange juice and a glass half-filled with the same sat on the counter, along with a mug of coffee. Another pot on the stove began to boil over, and Seth muttered a curse as he brought the pot to the sink. He saw her then, watching him, and a slow curl of heat began in the pit of her stomach.

No man should have eyes like Seth's. They were hooded and dark, making it difficult to read his thoughts, sinful in their sexuality and heartbreakingly beautiful to look into.

She hoped their daughter had his eyes.

He kept those eyes on her as he poured the water from the pot, as he removed the eggs and plopped them in a bowl filled with ice water to cool. And her entire body shivered with the need to go to him, to pull him to her for a kiss like she had last night.

"You called my office and told them I wouldn't be in." Rebecca forced her mouth into a scowl and planted her hands on her hips. "And you stayed the night without my permission."

"Guilty as charged." His back to her once again, Seth turned off the stove and moved the remaining pot to a cool burner. "I also made you hard-boiled eggs and oatmeal with a little cinnamon, some brown sugar. Why don't you settle yourself somewhere and we'll eat?"

"Seth," she said, working hard to keep the ice in her voice. "Look at me."

He did. His brows quirked in question, his mouth in teasing humor. "Are you set on punishing me, then? For making a few decisions without your input?"

The swirl of heat in her belly magnified, liquefied and all but whooshed through her blood. "You called my office," she repeated, "stayed the night and made me breakfast. And you want to know if I'm set on punishing you?"

"I did and I do."

His words, the very look and sound of him, sent Rebecca spiraling back in time. To another morning they stood here, in this kitchen, barefoot and hungry, laughing and kissing and touching as they threw together a quick meal of scrambled eggs and buttered toast.

Food they'd barely consumed before they returned to her bedroom. Rebecca hadn't been herself that weekend. She'd been a freer, happier, far more sexually aware version of herself. She discovered she wanted to be that woman again.

Going for sultry, she winked and said, "What type of punishment would you suggest?"

Stark, hungry desire darkened his eyes, deepened his voice. "Well, now. That's a good question." He took a step toward her, stopped. "No games, Rebecca. I—"

"I'm not playing." Her heart leaped as she made the claim. "My question is more along the lines if you still find me desirable."

He came to her then and cupped her face in his hands. His lips pressed against hers in a searching type of a kiss, soft and gentle in its exploration but insistent in his intent. He tasted of orange-spiced coffee, hot and sweet and tangy all at once. She drank in this taste, the feel of him, of his mouth against hers, and hers against his.

And she reveled in how such a simple action—the meeting of lips—could numb her rational brain into submission while every one of her physical senses exploded to life. She felt everything: the bristly roughness of Seth's unshaven jaw, the firm press of his hands on her face, the rocklike hardness of his muscular body, and the heat crackling and popping between them.

He tilted her face upward, so she had no choice but to stare into his eyes. They were deep and dangerous and filled with a raw, greedy type of need that stole the air clean from her lungs. A ball of heat gathered hard and fast between her legs and shot straight through her, searing her from the inside out, all but melting her with its strength.

"Yes," she said in answer to the unasked question simmering in his gaze. "I'm sure."

Grasping one of his hands, she led him to her bedroom. Without speaking, because words were *so* not necessary, she pulled his shirt off and ran her hands over his bare chest. Wherever she touched, muscles rippled and skin warmed. Her fingers drifted downward, following the silky line of slightly curly black hair that disappeared beneath the waistband of his jeans.

Eagerly and without an ounce of self-consciousness, she unclasped his jeans. One good yank edged them lower. She sucked in a breath and held it, enjoying the sight—the feel—of Seth. She swallowed hard and whispered feather-light strokes along his flat, firm stomach, creating a path to the mouthwatering, truly delicious angles of his hip bones.

He was pure, rugged masculinity. He was a wild, untamed land that made her heart pound and her blood hot and her soul hunger. She craved him in a primitive, intrinsic way that she didn't—or couldn't—completely comprehend.

But at the moment, she wasn't particularly concerned with comprehending anything. At the moment, the need she felt for Seth was all that mattered, all that drove her. Fully unzipping his jeans, she dragged them the rest of the way down. She hadn't meant for his boxers to follow the denim, but they did, and she figured that was fine. She'd have gotten to those soon enough.

"Becca," Seth whispered, his voice a tangle of desire and want, questions and concern.

Scraping his jaw with a flurry of small kisses, she said,

"I know what I want. This won't hurt the baby. Sex is allowed." With a sigh borne of anticipation, she wrapped her hand around the length, the hardness of him. "And this seems to state that you know what you want, as well."

"I know exactly what I want," he said, his voice a complex symphony of rough and hard and sweet and tender. Again, he cupped her cheeks and lifted her face toward his. "I want *you,* Becca. And more. Maybe more than what you're willing to give."

She knew what he meant. Of course, she knew. "Right now, I want us to make love to each other. I want to feel you inside of me."

"And what will you want after?"

The frantic beat of her heart slowed, but her desire for Seth remained strong, unrelenting. Closing her eyes, she drew in a breath. "There's a connection here, between us. You were right about that. I…don't know if I'll be able to move beyond my fears. So if you're looking for forever, I can't promise you that."

"I don't want a promise. All I want is for you to try." His thumb brushed along the soft curve of her lips. "For you to give us an honest chance. Can you do that?"

The thought of that—of simply *trying*—seemed terrifying. He might as well have asked her to take a flying leap out of an airplane with the assurance he'd catch her before she hit the ground. But what she felt for Seth was real. Had been real all along, which was why she ran from him to begin with. Truthfully, she'd already been thinking about running *before* her pregnancy test came back positive. Real scared her. Real meant…*real.*

Naturally, she meant to say no. She even meant to explain her reasons why. Because honestly, *nothing* had changed. But when she opened her eyes, she felt her chin dip in a small, tentative nod. And when she spoke, she heard herself saying, "I can do that. I can try. I *will* try."

It was her shirt that was being lifted up and off, then. Her pants that were tugged and pulled until they'd joined his in a pile on the floor. It was his hands that touched and caressed and made her shiver in delight, and his lips that brought tiny moans tumbling from her throat as they made their way over her neck, her shoulders, her breasts. The light glide of his fingers down her spine to the small of her back sent a long series of shuddering anticipation through her body.

With the same ease he'd shown last night, Seth lifted her in his arms and carried her to the bed. She wasn't embarrassed to admit that his strength, his ability to pick her up as if she weighed no more than what a loaf of bread might, made her feel incredibly, unbelievably female.

It also made her want him that much more.

Seth straddled her lower body with his. Leaning over, he kissed between her sensitive breasts and down to her swollen stomach, eliciting a trail of fire wherever his hungry mouth made contact. This—being with Seth—was everything she remembered and more.

So much more.

Flushed from head to toe, damn-near dissolving from his focused attention, Rebecca whimpered as he branded her one kiss, one glide of his tongue at a time. Long-fingered hands continually stroked until she was sure she would die from the need pumping through her.

How had she forgotten the energy, the electricity, that pulsed between them? How could she possibly have forgotten the way her body responded to his, the way his responded to hers? In that instant, she promised herself she'd never forget again. That she'd cherish what existed between them, regardless of what the future held, for the rest of her life.

Seth's lips came back to hers, and she stopped thinking.

Sinking into the sensations, she let his mouth devour hers. He kissed her as if he were starving and she were his sustenance. He tasted her as if she were ambrosia and he couldn't get enough, would never get enough. And when he lifted his eyes to hers, he looked at her as if she were the only woman in the world.

Gathering her close, so they were both sitting with their legs and arms wrapped around each other, he kissed her again. Slowly. Reverently. Possessively. One hand lifted her hair, the other skimmed and danced down her back, stopping in the shallow depression at the base. There, he slid his fingers under her bottom and pushed her forward until she felt the proof of his need, his desire, the hard length of his erection throbbing against her inner thigh.

And that, too, she basked in. That, too, made her feel powerful and alive, and so very feminine. She raised her hands to his shoulders and gave them a solid shove. They rolled until he was on his back and she was straddling him. She thought of the box of condoms sitting in her bedside table's drawer, almost reached over to get them, but decided they didn't need them. Seth would *never* put her at risk. She knew that to the core of her being, just as she knew the sky was blue and the grass was green. And if he had concerns, he would say so.

She slid herself down his body, shifted and…almost lost her balance. Embarrassment filtered into her desire. The last time she had Seth in her bed, she'd been slender and lithe and sexy. Now, as she stared at her enormous stomach, she felt awkward. And silly. And about as far away from sexy as a woman can get.

Before she could say these words, though, Seth teased her thighs with his fingertips, leaving goose bumps in their wake. Their gazes met and he winked, donned a lazy, seductive smile that seemed to state "do me, baby," and the hot flash of Rebecca's desire returned.

He wanted her. *He* found her sexy. What else mattered?

Seth grasped her hips. She settled herself on top of him, and the last bit of her awkwardness faded into nothing. With a cautious, silky sort of slide, he entered her, filling her in one gentle, languorous thrust. Her head fell back and her eyes half closed. This was delicious. This was Seth inside her. And it felt so right. So amazingly right.

He moved slowly, keeping their rhythm soft and languid with his hands firmly on her hips, guiding her...loving her. But she wanted more. She wanted *all of him*.

And dear God, she wanted all of him *now*.

Pressing her hips down harder, to take him in completely, she gasped in shock as her body tensed. She panted a breath, and then another, waiting for the intensity to subside, waiting for her body to stretch around him. But it was too much, too snug, too deep this far along in her pregnancy, and while not exactly painful, the feeling wasn't wholly comfortable, either.

As if Seth had read her mind, her expression, he lifted her hips and eased them to their sides, so they were once again facing each other. After a slight repositioning of their legs, hands and bodies, he entered her in the same careful slide as before. Her body opened and accepted him, tightened around him, and pulled him in deeper with each push of their hips.

Yes. This was glorious. This was...perfection.

His gorgeous, sinful eyes stayed on her, alert for any sign of distress or discomfort, keeping their pace slow and sensuous. And so very intimate. Their bodies moved as one and their breaths came faster. Pleasure, warm and sweet and satisfying, bounced from cell to cell and muscle to muscle, spreading through Rebecca like waves lapping at the shoreline, each one stronger than the last, each one pulling her closer to climax.

Seth captured her hands with his and held them tight. Their hips met again, over and over and over, and the waves of pleasure grew in speed and intensity. She let herself fall into the storm, lost in the sensations, lost in the smoldering depths of Seth's eyes. He swallowed and a groan spilled from his luscious mouth, her lips parted in a moan.

Her body screamed for more, so she drove her hips against his harder. His eyelids drooped, his body tensed and stilled, and his jaw went slack as he found his release. But oh...he was beautiful to look at in this moment. That spicy, seductive smile returned to his lips. He kept their rhythm, moving inside of her, bringing her one long, sweet stroke at a time to her finish.

Rebecca moaned again, unable to tear her vision away from his, unable to do anything but look and feel and move, when a brilliant burst of liquid power shattered through her, making her cry out Seth's name, leaving her limp and trembling and satisfied beyond reason.

And, as her soul drowned in the surety of Seth's gaze, of the promises she saw there, her heart stuttered to a stop, reset itself and flickered to life in the steady beat of a woman in love.

Seth carefully slid to the edge of the bed, not wanting to wake Rebecca. A quick once-over showed she still slept deeply. He feasted on the sight of her. From the delectable stretch of her legs to the rose blush of her nipples to her softly fanned out hair, she was glorious in her nakedness. And sexy as hell.

Was it weird he found a pregnant woman sexy? And beautiful? And so hot he'd take her again now if she was awake, willing and able? The thought gave him pause, as well as a dribble of concern. He'd known guys who had some out-there fetishes, and he didn't particularly relish the idea of joining any of those "special" clubs.

Okay, so her stomach was sort of large. Huge, really. Almost…blimplike. But seeing how Rebecca was close to eight months along, that was normal and to be expected. And looking at her stomach didn't fill him with desire or make him hard or anything. Rather, he felt…proud. And yeah, admittedly, sappy. *His* baby girl was in there, growing stronger day by day.

So that was good. That probably meant it wasn't pregnancy that turned him on, but Rebecca and the feelings he had for her. It was her eyes, her hair, the sound of her voice and the way she looked at him while he was deep inside her. He didn't think—no, he knew—he'd never before been so utterly connected to any other woman during sex.

Or, hell, after sex. Because the connection hadn't exactly faded now that she slept next to him. If anything, their bond— his love for her—had increased. Before, the thought of leaving his daughter behind had seemed impossible. Now, he couldn't imagine leaving Rebecca behind, either. Leaving both of them might just kill him.

Seth pulled the blanket over Rebecca's body to keep her warm. With a heavy sigh, he grabbed his jeans and shirt. He needed to go home, shower, get fresh clothes and return before Rebecca's appointment. A glance at the clock showed he had sufficient time, but he hated walking out the door while she slept. What if she woke before he returned?

Nah. That wouldn't do at all. If there was one concrete fact he knew about women it was to expect the unexpected. Whatever didn't make sense to a man would sure as shooting make sense to a woman. His absence could raise too many red flags. She might think he left unsatisfied. Or that he took off because he got scared. He could write a note, but hell, giving Rebecca time to herself didn't seem smart so soon after her decision to give them a shot. Seth shook his head, annoyed with himself.

He just didn't want to leave. Not today.

There wasn't any choice in the matter, then. He'd have to call someone and beg them to bring him what he needed. Phoning either of his parents was out of the question, and he didn't care for the idea of bothering Olivia. Grady and Jace were at work.

Dammit. That left him with one option.

Fastening his jeans, Seth went downstairs to call the pixie. And God help him, he actually hoped she was home and willing to help. Preferably without shoveling too much grief his way.

He made the call, said as little as possible, took a shower in the guest bathroom and put yesterday's clothes on again. Using a lather of soap and water and a disposable razor he found under the sink, he attempted shaving. And nicked himself twice.

Swearing, he tore off a couple of pieces of tissue and stuck them to the cuts to stop the bleeding. When that was dealt with, he opened the medicine cabinet in search of an extra toothbrush. No such luck, but he spied a bottle of mouthwash.

He gurgled the liquid and then bent over the sink to spit it out. A stream of mouthwash trickled down, soaking the tissue stuck to his skin and burning into the cuts left by the razor.

Seth jolted and cursed, tipped the open bottle of mouthwash in his hand, and dumped near-half of it on his wrinkled, white T-shirt. Bright green liquid spread into the fabric lightning fast, drenching it and his skin, and dripping down to the waistband of his jeans.

He ripped off the shirt, washed off the mess, cleaned his

jaw and neck for the second time and used more tissue to stop the fresh bleeding. After uselessly dabbing at the shirt with a wet washcloth, he put it back on and let out a long breath as he stared at himself in the mirror.

Hell and damnation, he was a mess. Stupid, maybe, but he didn't want to meet Rebecca's doctor looking like a bum on a bad day. It shouldn't matter. He *knew* it shouldn't matter. But it did, and that meant he needed the pixie to come through.

Twenty-five minutes later, Rebecca was still sleeping when Seth opened the door to a smirking Jocelyn. Her eyes rounded as she took in his appearance, her gaze dropping from his face to his neck to his green-splashed, damp shirt.

"Not a word," he warned. "Not one damn word."

"That's not happening. Not when you look as if you got into a fight with…with—" she leaned in and sniffed "—a candy cane. Why, you smell like Christmas, Seth!"

"It's mouthwash," he begrudgingly admitted. "The bottle…slipped."

"Before or after you cut yourself shaving?"

"After."

"Ouch." Jocelyn breezed by and plopped a large bag on the floor. "I'm here to save the day, but you owe me. I had to cancel my plans to help you out."

That almost made him feel bad. "Sorry, kid. Did you have a date or something?"

"Yeah, with Hawaiian Tropic, a book and an extra-large glass of iced tea. If you haven't noticed, it's unseasonably warm out today." She shoved her bare arm under his nose. The overpowering scent of coconut and summer assailed his senses. "Smells yummy, doesn't it? And now it's going to waste. So yeah, you owe me big time."

"For interrupting your day of sunbathing?" He moved toward the bag. "I'll buy you a new bottle of lotion. How's that?"

"Not nearly enough." Stepping in front of Seth, she sat

down on the arm of a chair, and swung her legs in front of the bag. "What happened last night, Seth? And where's my sister?"

"Rebecca is napping." Dealing with Jocelyn always left him frustrated and amused. It was an odd combination. "And nothing happened last night. I slept on the couch."

"Uh-huh. Sure you did." She gave him a long look. "Ah. I see. What happened *today,* then? After you woke up on the couch?"

His neck started to itch. "Why don't you give me the bag and you can get back to your sunbathing? Lots of good hours of 'unseasonably warm' sun left out there."

"You're embarrassed."

"Am not." Good God, when had he become a five-year-old again?

"Are too."

"Whatever happened—and I'm not saying anything did— is none of your business."

"Hmm." Jocelyn stared at him unblinking. He returned her stare, but he might have blinked once. Or twice. One of her brows shot up in amusement. With an impish expression, she said, "When you called, I was reading a book."

"You mentioned that." When the pixie continued to stare at him, he asked, "What book?"

"A romance. And I was just getting to the good part." Jocelyn's smirk returned, wider this time. "See, the heroine was dumped by the only guy she's ever had sex with. So she goes out to find a hottie to change that. And wouldn't ya know, she bumps into an excellent hottie right off the bat. Except the hottie has just made a bet with his friends that he can go a month without sex, but she doesn't know this, so she has to work real hard to get him into bed." Jocelyn pointed an accusing finger at Seth. "And you called at the exact moment she had her mouth on his—"

"Stop!" In no way did Seth want her to finish that sentence. "I...ah...can figure out the rest. But thanks for the book report."

Rising to her feet, Jocelyn patted his cheek. "You're so cute, getting all nervous at the slightest suggestion of sex."

"I'm not nervous. I'm...starting to think of you as my little sister, and talking about sex with my sister isn't cool." Close, but not quite accurate. He felt protective toward Jocelyn. "You're awfully tiny. Some men might try to take advantage of that. If some guy is ever a problem...pressuring you or something, you should tell me about that pronto."

"Wow." Jocelyn's teasing expression vanished. "That's kind of awesome. I always wanted a big brother to look out for me."

"As the baby in my family, I've always wanted *to be* a big brother," Seth admitted. "So I'm honored to take on that role for you. And seriously, Jocelyn, I don't want you getting hurt. So know I'll...ah...stand for you."

"Yeah?" she asked in a stunned voice. "You're serious?"

"Yeah. I am."

"Cool." They grinned at each other like idiots for a couple of seconds. Then, Jocelyn heaved a sigh and dropped her gaze to the shopping bag. "I sort of feel bad now, though."

"Why?"

"Well, see...none of my dad's clothes would fit you."

Uh-oh. "Okay."

"So I—" Her eyes downcast, she stubbed her toe against the carpeting, saying, "I guess you could say that I made an executive decision."

"Which would entail what, exactly?" Seth prodded.

"I went shopping. For you. See, I used to work at this men's store in the mall and I'm pretty good at guessing people's sizes."

"That was nice of you," Seth said cautiously. "What's the damage?"

"Let's call this my treat since... Well, my taste in fashion is *unique*."

Oh, hell. Seth looked at the bag and then back at Jocelyn. "What did you buy me?"

"Normal stuff. Basically, your typical, everyday wardrobe." Avoiding his gaze, she whispered, "If you're a thirteen-year-old girl."

"What?" Seth grabbed the bag and dumped its contents on the chair. At first, it didn't look so bad. The jeans were lighter than he liked, but he could live with them for one afternoon. And the cartoon covered boxers were silly, but no one had to see those. But then he saw an edge of pale pink sticking out from underneath the jeans. "You bought me a *pink* shirt?"

"Pink can be manly. I've seen lots of guys wearing pink shirts," she argued weakly. "But...you won't care much about the color in a second." At those words, Seth reached for the shirt. Jocelyn backtracked toward the door. "Thank you for that big brother thing. It means a lot. But I should take off and...get back to my romance novel."

"Stop," he said, yanking the shirt free. Once he got a good look at it, he shuddered. "Tell me this is a joke. Tell me you have another shirt—a *normal* shirt—in your car."

"Well, it is a joke. But no, I don't have another shirt in my car."

"I can't wear this."

"Why not?" Jocelyn asked with a hint of her typical sarcastic wit. "It will fit, won't it?"

"Jocelyn," he said slowly, striving toward calmness. "This is not a man's shirt."

"I picked it up in the men's department."

"It has a castle and flowers and a *rainbow,*" he sputtered. "And a...a...purple horse with a horn."

"That would be a unicorn," she said, her voice muffled with restrained laughter.

"A friggin' unicorn!" Seth scowled in disbelief. "You bought me a shirt with a unicorn?"

"I certainly didn't buy it for me."

He shook the T-shirt and a puff of sparkly stuff floated in the air. "Glitter," he muttered. And it was rubbing off on his hand. Dropping the shirt fast, he tried to brush off the sparkles. "Men do not wear pink and violet shirts with glittery unicorns!"

"The color you're referring to is lavender. Violet is darker and much more vibrant, with more blue tones than say—"

"You did not find this pink and *lavender* shirt in the men's department." Why he was arguing that point, he didn't know. It seemed important. "No way."

"I did." She shrugged. "Though it was the only one there, and it sort of looked as if someone had left it…like they didn't want to return the shirt to the proper department."

His frustration at the situation—at the damn shirt—turned into faint humor. Closing his eyes for a second, he let out a breath. "I either have to wear a scratch-and-sniff, peppermint-mouthwash-stained shirt to Rebecca's doctor's appointment or I have to wear *this*."

"Oh. I…didn't know you were going with her today. I thought you'd be hanging out here." Jocelyn held out her hand, instantly contrite. "Give it back. I'll get you something else before you have to leave. I'm sorry."

"There isn't time. I have to wake up Becca, get some food in her and we have to take off." Reality set in, along with a strong dose of exasperated affection. "Hell, this really is what it's like to have an annoying little sister, isn't it?"

"I guess." She stubbed her toe against the carpet again. "You're seriously not mad?"

"I don't get mad," he joked. "I get even. Just wait until your birthday rolls around, kid."

"Well," she said, reaching into the pocket of her shorts. "Maybe this will help. I found it after the baby shower, before I went home that day." She pulled out her hand and offered him the engagement ring Rebecca had tossed in the rosebushes.

Accepting the ring, he stared at it for a second. "Why?"

"Originally, I thought I'd sell it. To help Rebecca out with some extra money after my niece is born." Jocelyn shrugged again. "I didn't like you very much at first. But once I understood everything that happened, I got to thinking. And now... Well, now I think you should propose again. The *right* way, though. When she's ready."

"So the ring hasn't been out there this whole time?"

"Yeah, but Rebecca doesn't know."

"That could prove interesting," he mumbled. Hearing the unmistakable sound of the shower swishing on upstairs, he stuck the ring in his pocket and ushered Jocelyn to the door. "Thanks for returning the ring, but I still plan on getting even for that shirt."

"Cool," she said as she walked outside. "I'd be disappointed if you weren't."

Seth held up the shirt for another look. Yeah, it was bad. So bad that if the guys at the base saw him in this, he'd never live it down. Maybe if he hurried Rebecca along, they'd have time to stop at his parents' place before the appointment.

Otherwise, he'd wear the mouthwash shirt. Because no way, no how... *Oh, hell.*

If, for whatever reason, Rebecca came down those stairs feeling uncomfortable about what had happened between them, then seeing sparkly unicorns and rainbows on his chest would break the ice. How could it not? She'd surely laugh, and he loved hearing her laugh.

Before Seth could think his way out of it, he took off his T-shirt and put on the girly shirt. Now, despite what thoughts might be mucking up Rebecca's head, the first thing she'd do when she saw him was smile. And that simple fact right there somehow made even the horrifying humiliation of glitter worthwhile.

Chapter Nine

"What about Claire?" Rebecca asked Seth early Wednesday evening. She was stretched out on her sofa, feeling very much the lady of leisure with a baby-name book propped on her belly and her feet on Seth's lap. "It's French and means illustrious. That's nice, isn't it?"

"Sure," he said easily, rubbing his thumbs up the sole of her left foot. "I dated a Claire once. She was very nice." He winked at her. "Memorable, too."

"Okay, that's a no for Claire." Rebecca crossed off the name with a heavy slash of her red pen and attempted to ignore the flash of jealousy. "All ex-girlfriend names are out."

"Didn't say she was my girlfriend." The corners of his mouth twitched into a grin. "Just that she was nice and memorable."

"Hmm." Somehow, over the past two days, they'd fallen into an *almost* comfortable routine. Odd, seeing how Rebecca had awakened from her nap on Monday in the firm grip of icy fear. She *couldn't* love Seth. Hadn't she sworn off loving him eons ago? Indeed, she had.

Determined to clear the air, to renounce her feelings as nonsense, she descended the stairs to confront Seth. She found him in the kitchen preparing a meal. And again, deep longing struck as she watched. When she caught sight of the ridiculous shirt he wore, her fear and her intent dissolved into hysterical, tear-inducing laughter.

Good grief, he'd looked silly.

But he kept the shirt on through the doctor's appointment, grinning at her every time she giggled. Even her doctor had laughed once she heard the story—though Rebecca did have a few choice words to say to Jocelyn. Her sister had shrugged it off, saying that she and Seth had reached an understanding. What that meant, Rebecca wasn't sure.

But, she thought as she skimmed her pen down the next page of names, the fact that Seth had worn the shirt told her a lot about the man. When Rebecca was a child, her dad used to let her paint his nails on a fairly regular basis. Sure, he always cleaned off the polish pretty fast, but the important part was that he was secure enough in his masculinity to play with his daughter.

Thanks to that shirt, Rebecca knew Seth would be the same with *their* daughter. Now, her desire to protect herself not only warred with her love for him—which she'd given up denying—but with a future she was desperately beginning to want. So, although it terrified her, she was trying to stick with what she told him—that she'd try.

The past few days had shown a slice of how their life might look if they managed to cross their many hurdles. After Monday's appointment, they'd gone for a walk, had dinner on her back deck and spent an hour watching television. Seth hadn't stayed over, but he was waiting for her when she came home on Tuesday. Their activities that night mirrored Monday's. Today, he surprised her by having flowers delivered at her office. And now, they were cuddled on the couch like an old married couple, trying to find the perfect name for their daughter.

Beneath the ever-present fear, she'd enjoyed sharing her evenings with Seth. Even so, she'd held back. A low buzz of unspoken questions existed on the fringes of everything they said and did. Unprepared to answer those questions, to get into any conversation that dealt with the future of their relationship, Rebecca avoided the openings Seth gave her and diverted his attention whenever she thought he was raring up to plunge in.

Cowardly, yes. But also easier. Was it so wrong to enjoy the simplicity of being with Seth for now? She didn't think so. Especially when thinking ahead brought her face-to-face with all of the sensible reasons why she should push away.

"How about Cordelia?" she asked, instilling a cheery note into her tone. "It has an old-fashioned flair to it, don't you think?"

"Cordelia," Seth repeated, as if giving the name a practice run. "I don't know, sweetheart. Seems too big of a mouthful for a tiny baby."

"She won't always be tiny. Or a baby. But okay, I'll keep looking." Letting go of her left foot, he picked up her right. Sighing in contentment, she closed her eyes when he started to rub in deep strokes just above her heel. "That's heavenly. You have no idea."

"I have some idea," he said, his voice low and delicious. "Or I wouldn't be doing it."

"Every stroke is like a miniature orgasm." She opened one eye. "I'm not joking."

"Didn't think you were." Seth continued to rub his thumbs in a circular pattern as he moved up her foot. "Glad this feels good, though."

Huh. She'd expected a teasing, sexy type of response. Perhaps even a quick trip upstairs for some not-so-miniature orgasms. Rebecca opened her other eye. He watched her intently, his expression solemn and searching. Serious.

Raring up to ask her something, she guessed. So she pretended to be oblivious and used the open book to hide her face. "Oh, here's a good one! What do you think of Darlene? Almost sounds like 'Darling,' doesn't it?"

"I like it." Seth exhaled a soft sigh. "But I'm not sold on it. We should keep looking."

"Oh, we will." Rebecca forced a chuckle and pushed her foot into his chest. "Our daughter's name is in this book somewhere."

"Then we'll find it." Seth dropped a light kiss on her toe. "Jocelyn's going with you to the birthing class tomorrow night, right?"

"Um, yeah. That's what we decided, anyway. Why?"

"Well, last weekend I spent some time with Jace and Melanie, but haven't really done much with Grady and Olivia yet," Seth said slowly. "They invited me over and I'd like to go, but wanted to be sure you were all set with the class. And that you'd be okay for the evening."

"I'm all set." *For the evening?* As in, she wouldn't see him *at all* tomorrow? "Um… Will you be stopping in later? Should I hold dinner or…?"

"They invited me for dinner. As to later…I don't know, sweetheart."

"Well, if you don't want to come over, then—"

"Why wouldn't I want to?" Seth grazed his finger along her ankle. "Grady has a few of the ball games I missed on his DVR. It's sort of a thing for us, a way to catch up. I'm just not sure how late it'll go, and you need your rest."

Every word made sense. His reasoning was practical and considerate. But what Rebecca heard was "I want a night without you." And while she *knew* she was being ridiculous, it hurt. A lot. Sitting up straight, she nodded and gripped the book tight.

"That sounds fun! And a night to myself is exactly what I need. Besides," she said with a toss of her hair, "we don't have to spend all of our free time together. I mean, I'm busy for part of Saturday. I...made plans with Melanie and Olivia. Felicia and Jocelyn might join us, too."

"That beauty day thing, right?"

"That's right." Her voice cracked, which upset her more. Aargh. She hated how, along with her physical changes, pregnancy had her emotions jumping from one extreme to another. "P-Please tell Grady I said hi. Olivia, too, though I'll see her on Saturday."

And then, for no reason at all, she burst into tears.

"Hey, now." Seth slid over to her and pulled the book from her hands. "Why the tears? This really is about hanging with my family. I was gone awhile and they missed me. But you gotta know, sweetheart, spending my evenings with you is always preferable."

"I get it. I really do," she whispered. "I don't know what's wrong with me."

"There is nothing wrong with you."

As if to prove his point, he set the book on the coffee table and brought his mouth to hers. She leaned in closer, allowing herself to fall into the slow and drugging way Seth kissed her, loving the way this—*he*—made her feel, and tried not to think about how empty this house—her life and her heart—would feel when he was no longer here.

Because right now, in this instant, Seth *was* here. Raising her chin, she looked into his eyes. "I want you," she murmured, succumbing to the need twisting inside of her. "Will you stay with me tonight? All night?"

Twining his fingers into her hair, Seth said, "Aw, sweetheart, you know I will."

Then, his mouth recaptured hers and she quit thinking altogether.

Seth arrived at his brother's place in Beaverton, a suburb of Portland, an hour before he expected Grady to be home from work. He wanted to spend some one-on-one time with his sister-in-law. Naturally, he called first, to ascertain that Olivia didn't mind his showing up early. She hadn't, so here he was.

They settled in the living room. Pictures of his late nephew, Cody, were scattered on the end tables, causing Seth's heart to shudder in fresh grief. It seemed beyond wrong to come into this house without a little boy barreling into his arms the second he walked through the door.

Swallowing to lessen the tightness in his throat, Seth said, "I miss him, Olly. I *hate* that he isn't here right now, quizzing me about what it's like to fly, and how the clouds look up close, and—" Here, he broke off, unable to continue.

"I know." Olivia's eyes softened with the sheen of tears. "I miss him, too. Every single day. I'm learning that will never go away. But…he was amazing, wasn't he?"

"Best kid I've ever known." Seth shook his head, feeling like a louse for upsetting Olivia. "I shouldn't have brought him up. Talking about Cody is difficult for me, so I can't imagine what it's like for you." And God help him, he hoped he'd *never* know that kind of pain.

"I like talking about my son, Seth." Her fingers dipped beneath the collar of her shirt to grasp the charms—three tiny gold figures embellished with birthstones, representing a family—on her necklace. "Even if I do get a little weepy."

"Grady told me about that," Seth said, nodding toward the necklace. "How he and Cody bought that for you…and how Grady saved it until this past Christmas to give you."

"I saved the box and the wrapping paper it came in," she admitted. "The tag, too. Cody colored on them, you see. So they were as much a gift as this, as much a miracle to receive."

"I get that." What Seth wanted to ask was how she stood it, how she dealt with the fact that her son was gone because a stranger drank too much and decided in his intoxicated state that he was capable of operating a car. Too harsh, though, so he went with, "How are you, really?"

"Ninety percent of the time, I'm wonderful."

"And the other ten percent?"

"Varies," she said in a hushed tone. "Some days are worse than others. Every now and then, a really bad one sneaks up on me. But…as much as I wish I could change the past and bring Cody back, I—" She bit her bottom lip in thought. "Grady and I are where we are supposed to be. We're creating new memories, but we're remembering to stop and celebrate our old memories, too. They're sweet and beautiful, and help keep Cody with us."

"Must be hard at times," Seth said. "But it's incredible you're able to do that."

"I have Grady to thank for a lot of that." Resting her hands on top of her rounded stomach, she smiled. "Your brother *taught* me how to do that."

"I'm so damn glad you two worked things out," Seth said. "You're a part of my family, Olivia. And that's forever in my book. I guess…I guess what I'm getting at is that I love you like a sister. Not a sister-in-law."

"And I've been worried sick about you." Olivia inhaled a quick breath. "*I'm* so glad you're home safe. Why can't you fly commercially?"

"Someday, maybe." Seth thought of Rebecca, of her loss. Of Jesse. "Maybe sooner rather than later. And I wish you all would believe me when I tell you my job isn't that dangerous." He shrugged, knowing he was fighting a losing battle on that front. "I haven't made any decisions yet, though I'll have to soon. But I am sorry for worrying you."

"I was teasing, Seth. We're all so proud of you, and sure we worry, but we want you to be happy. Do what's right for you."

"And what about what's right for Rebecca and my daughter?" Because, despite the relative safety, his job often required him to be gone for extended periods of time. Seth held up a hand. "Never mind. I don't really want you to answer that."

"Good, because I can't. Only you and Rebecca can figure that one out."

Desperate for a change of subject, Seth leaned over and patted Olivia's stomach. "Boy or girl, this kid is so lucky to have you and Grady for parents."

Olivia landed a soft kiss on his cheek, saying, "Your kid is pretty lucky, too, having you for her father. Don't forget that, okay?"

"I hope I can be even half the father that my dad and Grady are."

"You already love her, Seth. So you're already more than halfway there." Using his knee as an anchor, Olivia pushed herself to a stand. "Now, I need to finish dinner. Feel like helping?"

"I can do that," he said, rising to his feet. "Or you can take it easy and I can cook."

She arched an eyebrow. "And trust you in my kitchen all alone? I don't think so. But," she said with a tug on his arm, "I have many fun jobs for you. Come and see."

Enchiladas were on the menu, along with Spanish rice and some type of a cold, but spicy, cucumber soup that Seth didn't think he'd like, but ended up having two bowlfuls. After eating, Seth insisted on cleaning up, so Grady and Olivia could have some time to themselves before the men hunkered down in front of the television.

Olivia agreed. He resisted teasing her about how it was okay to leave him alone in her kitchen to clean, just not to cook. She looked tired and kept rubbing the small of her back, so really, he wanted her to rest.

When the kitchen was spotless, Seth grabbed a couple of beers and went to the family room. Grady joined him a few minutes later, easily catching the bottle Seth tossed.

"Olivia okay?" Seth asked, twisting the top off his beer.

"Yup. Tired, is all. She's lying down with a book." Grady steadied his gaze on Seth. "How's Rebecca doing? Was real nice to meet her, by the way."

"She's good. Drops to part-time at work next week, which is a relief." Seth picked at the label on his bottle. "I don't think she sleeps very well most nights. Has these dark smudges under her eyes all the time. Worries me."

"It's natural this late in the game, so I wouldn't worry too much." Grady swallowed a mouthful of beer. "Olly's sleep is interrupted more often these past few weeks. Either she's uncomfortable or the baby's activity, kicking and such, wakes her."

Seth nodded. Logical enough, but he still wished Rebecca slept better. Another pregnancy-related question came to mind, so he asked that. When Grady answered, Seth had the next question ready to go. This went on for close to thirty minutes before Seth's stored up concerns and curiosities ran dry.

Fortunately for him, his brother was an understanding and receptive audience. They sat quietly, companionably for a few minutes, before Grady picked up the remote.

"We good for the game now?" he asked. "Or…?"

"I'm good," Seth confirmed. Well…he did have another concern. One additional bit of information he'd like verified, but he wasn't entirely comfortable asking. "All set."

Grady coughed and gave him the I-know-better-so-spill

look. "You're sure?" Aiming the remote at the television, he said, "Last chance, bro. Once I hit play, I'm not pausing."

"Nah, you'd pause it."

"Try me." Grady brought up the DVR menu, scrolled to the appropriate game, and hovered his finger over the play button. "One. Two. Th—"

"Okay! You win." Seth strung the words together in his head. Nope, there wasn't any way not to sound idiotic. "Is it strange or…I don't know, *fetishlike,* to be…attracted to a pregnant woman? *Strongly* attracted, I mean."

"Depends," Grady said evenly, as if Seth had asked about the weather. "Are you talking about my pregnant woman or *your* pregnant woman? Because if it's Olivia—"

"No! Damn, Grady, you think I'm lusting after Olivia?" Seth shook his head vehemently, wanting to strike out that notion fast. "She's like my sister. I… No. *Never.*"

"So *your* pregnant woman, then."

"Yes. God, yes."

"Alrighty then," Grady said without missing a beat. "Any other pregnant women besides Rebecca that you're drooling…ah, *strongly attracted* to?"

"No." Seth drained the rest of his beer. "Only her."

"Then you're fine," Grady said with a dismissive shrug. "*Now* can we watch the game?"

"Please, let's watch the game." Even though Seth had reached the same conclusion, it was a relief to have confirmation from his brother. "Want me to grab a couple more beers first?"

"If you're bunking on the couch tonight, sure."

"Planned on it."

"Good." Grady waved the remote in the air. "But hurry it along. I might be the boss, but I still have to work tomorrow."

"Give it up. Olivia already told me you're staying home."

Seth grinned. "Apparently, you've *missed* me and have been looking forward to this and have talked of little else."

"I don't know what you're rambling on about," Grady grumbled good-naturedly. "Just go get the beers, will ya?"

Seth bounded up the stairs that led to the kitchen. Over his shoulder, he said, "It's cool, bro. I've missed hanging with you, too."

Rebecca breathed in the balmy afternoon air, sipped her fruit smoothie and sighed in contentment. Felicia sat on her left, Jocelyn on her right, and Olivia and Melanie were on the opposite side of the large, round table they'd claimed in the flower-filled, sunny courtyard.

Four and a half hours of beauty treatments had left Rebecca in a terrific, world-is-my-oyster type of mood. And she couldn't forget last night's hotter than hot sex with Seth, either. That definitely contributed to her current state of boneless, satiated relaxation.

Gracious, she felt good. Even the sporadic tightening in her lower back wasn't going to get her down. Not today. Not when she was flat out enjoying herself.

By mutual agreement, the women had decided to stop for lunch after leaving Melanie's mom's salon. Well, more of a small, intimate day spa, really. They'd ended up here, at a newly opened bistro on the outskirts of downtown Portland. If not for the sound of cars zipping by, Rebecca would almost believe they were in the backyard of a private residence.

"This place is great," she said to no one in particular. "And Melanie, your mother and her employees are miracle workers."

"She'll be so pleased to hear that." Melanie stabbed her fork into her salad, spearing a cherry tomato. Sunlight hit her engagement ring, bringing a glow of sparkles to the diamond. "Mom only recently added the spa services, so she's still nervous about the changes."

"Well, I think it's wonderful," Rebecca said faintly, staring at Melanie's ring and thinking of *Seth's* ring. Right then and there, she resolved to find it. The next opportunity that presented itself—meaning, when Seth wasn't at her house—she'd swallow her stupid, useless pride and dig through the rosebushes. What she'd do with the ring then remained... foggy, but she could worry about that later.

"I can't figure out how your mom talked me into this," Felicia said to Melanie in a shaky voice. She fingered her now chin-length auburn locks—a somewhat drastic change from her former shoulder-length, brown hair—and shuddered. "I remember saying I wanted a trim, and then she said stuff about cheekbones and eyes and warm tones, and before I knew it, I...agreed."

Melanie blinked. "Are you upset?"

With a slow shake of her head, Felicia grinned. "I think I like having a new look." She glanced worriedly at Rebecca. "This suits me, right?"

"Hmm." Rebecca studied Felicia carefully, knowing her friend wouldn't believe her if she answered too quickly. "Does saucy hot with a side of sizzle suit you?"

Felicia's hazel eyes rounded. After a moment's deliberation, she laughed. "I think it just might. Oh, this is so fun! Thank you for inviting me."

"This *is* fun, isn't it?" Olivia tore off a bite-size piece of bread from the basket. "I haven't had a girls' day out in forever. We should make this a regular outing, say once a month or so."

Everyone started chatting about the possibility, reviewing their individual schedules, discussing the need for babysitters for Olivia and Rebecca when the babies were born, and ending with Melanie's promise to make the salon arrangements with her mother.

Through it all, Jocelyn remained quiet and poked at her French fries, alternately breaking them into pieces and dunking them into the glop of catsup on her plate. Rebecca reached under the table to squeeze her sister's knee.

"What's wrong?" she asked softly. When Jocelyn looked at her with big, sad green eyes, Rebecca tried to coax a smile by saying, "Don't tell me you're already regretting those crazy purple streaks in your hair?"

"*Violet* streaks." Jocelyn tugged at one of the chunks framing her face. "And it's temporary, so no regrets."

"Then what?"

"I'm just now realizing how much I'm going to miss you when I leave in August," Jocelyn said in a near-whisper. "Everything will change. Maybe I'm not as ready as I thought. Maybe when I come home again, you'll be too busy—" Pausing, she rolled her eyes. "I'm being a dork. I'll miss you, that's all."

"You are being a dork," Rebecca said lightly, matching her tone to her sister's, "because I will always have time for you. And I know leaving home is scary, but it's also exciting. You'll love Stanford, and you *are* ready."

Felicia, catching most of the conversation, scooted her chair away from the table and leaned behind Rebecca to say, "Your sister has already asked if I'm willing to babysit next March, so she can visit you for your birthday. And I already told her yes."

"Yeah?" Jocelyn brightened immediately. "That's so cool! By then, you'll be ready for a mommy vacation and I'll have settled in and will know all the best places to take you. Oh! And if you bring Seth, you could maybe extend your visit, make it part romantic getaway."

"That's a nice thought," Rebecca said carefully, aware of

Olivia's and Melanie's gazes on her. "But too far away to plan right this second."

"You'll be together," Jocelyn said with an assurance that sent a burst of apprehension pummeling through Rebecca's system, followed by the slow, relentless fizzle of hope. "Mom and I both think so, and even Dad likes him."

"Dad likes Seth? Wow." Mitchell Carmichael tended to view any men dating his daughters as the enemy, so this was…interesting news.

"I'm not surprised," Olivia said as she stirred her straw in her glass to break up a chunk of melted-together ice. "Foster men are…very likeable."

"Charismatic, too," Melanie added. "Not to mention funny, loyal, intelligent—"

"Ridiculously good-looking," Olivia said. "Intense. Courageous. Determined."

"Built," Jocelyn said with a grin. "*Very* nicely built. All three of them."

Rebecca sighed wistfully. "And they have sinful eyes. Seth's remind me of the richest, blackest coffee with the tiniest splash of cream."

"Cinnamon," Olivia said, sighing, as well. "When I look into Grady's eyes, I think of cinnamon and spice…and I just about melt."

"You're both wrong." Melanie's cheeks reddened. "Well, maybe not wrong, but Jace's eyes don't look anything like cinnamon or coffee. They're…warm and chocolaty," she said with a sigh of her own. "Dark and smooth and luscious."

"This isn't fair." Felicia slapped her hand on the table, startling everyone. "I haven't met Seth, and I certainly haven't met…Grady and Jace? I need pictures so I can sigh, too." Brows arched, she held out her hand toward Melanie and Olivia. "I know you have pictures."

"Of course we have pictures," Olivia said, pulling her purse on her lap. "Get yours out, too, Mel. Between both of us, we probably have shots of all three of them."

In less than a minute, photos were pushed across the table. Felicia shoved her plate aside to spread them in front of her. And, if Rebecca wasn't mistaken, her friend's forthcoming sigh was filled with a mix of envy, disbelief and not a little lust.

"Holy cow," Felicia all but wheezed. "I need a Foster brother. Tell me there's a fourth brother, please. Pretty please? Black-sheep of the family is fine. Poor is fine. As long as he has this gene pool, I'm good to go."

Laughing, Olivia said, "Sorry, Felicia. There are some male cousins, though. Sadly, they don't live in Oregon. Grady's uncle moved his entire family to Colorado when the boys were little. I've only met them once, when they were here for a family reunion."

"Do they look like this?" Felicia jabbed her finger against a photo that had all three of the Foster brothers lounging on the front porch of a Victorian house.

"Actually, there is a strong family resemblance," Olivia confirmed. "But…I haven't seen them for years. So I have no idea what's going on with them now."

"Well, that settles it." Felicia gave one last, longing look at the photos before returning them to Melanie and Olivia. "I'm relocating to Colorado."

"Good idea, Felicia," Rebecca teased. "Moving to another state based on a gene pool."

"It's a delicious gene pool. Well worth it, in my opinion," her friend argued.

"In addition to the deliciousness, the Foster men are also stubborn," Olivia warned, tucking the photos into her wallet. "I'm not talking your everyday variety of stubborn, either."

"I can attest to that," Melanie said. "And sometimes, Jace

is… Well, let's just say we've had a ton of conversations about including *me* in making decisions that involve *us both*."

"Amen to that." Rebecca finished off her smoothie, wiped her mouth and said, "Seth ordered—yes, *ordered*—me to marry him. Told me to pack my bags and we were driving to Vegas. And he meant it. Absolutely expected I'd salute and say, 'Sir. Yes, sir!'"

"That's the problem with the Foster men," Olivia said with a small, sweet, secretive sort of smile. "They decide they want something, and—"

"They won't stop until they get it," Melanie finished off. She raised her empty glass to Rebecca in a faux toast. "You might not know it yet, but you're as good as caught."

"Hmm," Jocelyn said in a dreamy voice. "Rebecca Foster. I like it, sis."

Rebecca shivered when goose bumps—a million of them from the feel of it—exploded into being on her arms, legs… heck, her entire body. An invisible but unmistakable force seemed to be pulling her down a path she hadn't yet decided she had the courage to take.

That annoyed her. Rebecca disliked being pushed into anything. *She* was in power of her own life, no one else. But then, out of nowhere, a picture of Seth wearing that unicorn shirt invaded her mind, softened her heart and dispelled the mad she'd had brewing.

"They know how to love," she said, almost surprised when she heard her own voice. "The Foster brothers…they *know* how to love."

Olivia, Melanie, and Rebecca exchanged knowing glances, shared a sigh and collapsed in their respective chairs. Then, one by one, they fanned their faces with their hands.

"Colorado, here I come," Felicia muttered as she, too, collapsed in her chair. A few minutes of silence passed before she aimed her vision at Olivia. "It occurs to me that Colorado is a large state. I will need an address."

"Sure," Olivia said, going along with the joke. "I'll get right on that."

They spent another hour or so talking and laughing. By the time Rebecca headed for home, all of her thoughts were on Seth. He'd promised a surprise for tonight, and for once, the idea of a surprise made her…happy. So much so, she couldn't wait to see what he had planned.

Chapter Ten

Seth simultaneously yanked at his tie and fidgeted in his seat, wishing the waiter would hurry up already and return his credit card and receipt. Bringing Rebecca to a fancy, candlelit, soft-music-playing-in-the-background Italian restaurant—one that Grady had recommended, no less—was supposed to be the beginning of a knock-it-out-of-the-ballpark romantic evening.

Except Rebecca had seemed uncomfortable and distracted from the second he picked her up all the way through dinner. Which she'd barely eaten four bites of. Seth knew this for fact, because he'd counted every lift of the fork to her gorgeous berry-painted mouth. Now, she was in the restroom "freshening up," and he was rethinking his plans for the remainder of their date.

A couple of blankets were stashed in the trunk of his car, along with a bottle of sparkling grape juice. Seeing how they were near the South Park Blocks, a twelve-block stretch of city park in the heart of downtown Portland, his thought had been to take an early evening stroll. Perhaps find a picturesque spot to lay out the blanket, so they could relax and... hell, do whatever couples did on blankets in the middle of a park.

Cuddle, he supposed. He'd never really thought of himself as a cuddly type of a guy, especially in public, especially when wearing a suit he'd borrowed from Grady. But for Rebecca, he'd cuddle. And, yeah, he'd probably like it. Unfortunately, the lady didn't appear to be enjoying herself, so Seth was having second thoughts on the park, the stroll and the blanket.

He'd also considered broaching the topic of Jesse, of Rebecca's fears regarding Seth's career. But that particular subject would suck the romance clean out of *any* night, so he'd stuck that on the back burner, as well. They needed to have that conversation, though. Soon. Before she made a decision without hearing him out.

Lost in thought, he patted the suit jacket pocket where the diamond ring resided. The evening's plans hadn't definitely included another stab at a proposal, but he kept the ring with him all of the time now. That way, if a moment felt right, he'd have it close at hand.

Tonight did not, in any way whatsoever, feel right.

The waiter approached with the credit card folder and Rebecca's leftovers, gave the normal thanks-for-joining-us spiel and hurried off to see to another table. Seth was replacing his credit card in his wallet when Rebecca carefully slid into her chair.

"How are you feeling, sweetheart?" Seth asked, concerned by what he saw.

"I'm feeling like a moose," Rebecca joked. "But other than that, just dandy."

"You're beautiful and sexy and do not resemble a moose."

All true. The long, clingy black dress she wore hugged her
curves and showed off the perfect amount of tantalizing cleav-
age. She was, to Seth's way of thinking, beyond exquisite.
"You also look a little pale. And you didn't eat very much."

"I think the baby has shifted or something, because I
haven't had much of an appetite all day. But the food was
wonderful, and I love that you thought to bring me here."

"You're sure that's all it is?"

"Sure enough. Remember, I've never been pregnant before,
so this is all as new to me as it is to you." Reaching across
the small table, she grasped his hand. "I'm okay. I promise
to tell you instantly if that changes."

"Good." He kissed the back of her hand. "I had planned a
walk in the park, but maybe we should head home and relax
for the rest of the evening."

"You planned a walk in the park?" she asked, her warm
and sultry voice holding a hint of anticipation. "Oh, that
sounds…romantic. I'd like to go."

Seth studied her, noting the gleam in her eyes and the new
flush of excitement coloring her cheeks. Letting go of her
hand, he nodded and patted his pocket again, felt the outline
of the ring and smiled. Perhaps there was some romance left
in this evening, after all.

"Then, darling," he said with a wink, "that's exactly what
we'll do."

They left the restaurant to stroll hand in hand through two
and a half blocks of the twelve that made up the city park.
Along the way, they chatted casually about possible baby
names and stopped here and there to appreciate some of the
artwork the park featured.

Mostly, Rebecca had enjoyed the walk, even with the per-
sistent, nagging ache in her lower back. They were currently
nestled on a thick, wool blanket that Seth had spread out on

the grass, in a clearing between several of the park's massive elms. Rebecca was cradled between Seth's legs, using his body to support hers, while he supported his against a tree trunk.

Every aspect of this evening should have filled her with a romantic glow. It hadn't because an internal debate had raged all through dinner. As she picked at her fettuccine, she came to the undeniable conclusion that to truly take power over her own life, she needed to learn more about *Seth's* life.

She had allowed fear to be her guiding force, which was bad enough. Worse, she'd allowed *uninformed* fear to be the motivating factor in a decision she regretted over and above any other decision she'd ever made. It was a huge mistake, almost beyond redemption.

Learning from that mistake meant she *had* to become informed before contemplating a future with Seth. But yeah, doing so scared her.

In addition, there were practical elements that needed to be taken into consideration. Her job was here. His job was wherever the Air Force sent him. Everything she'd ever known and loved were all in Portland. Except now she loved Seth, and Seth couldn't make his home here. To really *be with* him, she'd have to give up everything *and* face the fears that haunted her.

The whole of it might be a good deal more than she was capable of, especially with a child to raise. But she wouldn't know—couldn't know—until she began the journey.

And she might as well get started now.

"I know you fly for the Air Force but I don't really know what that entails," she said in what she hoped passed for a light, breezy tone. "Maybe we could talk about that for a few minutes? If you're allowed to, I mean."

"Sweetie, I'm not a spy." Seth's fingers, which had been playing with her hair, stilled. "I've been wanting to discuss my job. What is it you'd like to know?"

"Um." A spasm of pain flickered in Rebecca's back, followed by painless tightening in her stomach. Braxton Hicks, she figured, brought on by the walk. "What do you fly?"

"I pilot C-17s. Or, officially, the C-17A Globemaster." He kissed the top of her head. "This might disappoint you, but C-17s are transport aircraft. So if you were thinking I'm the real-life version of Tom Cruise from *Top Gun,* that isn't the case."

"Oh." Huh. "Well, I know that, silly. Tom Cruise's character wasn't in the Air Force."

"True." Seth's laugh had a forced ring to it. "But that wasn't what I meant."

Pressing her head against Seth's chest, she tried to relax. "What do you transport?"

"Troops, obviously. Equipment and weapons." He squeezed her shoulder, and when he spoke again, she heard his pride in every softly uttered syllable. "C-17s are called on for tactical airlift, humanitarian aid, airdrop and medical evacuation missions throughout the world."

"You really love what you do, don't you?"

"I get to fly, which is all I've ever wanted, but it's something really special to do what you love and know you're making a difference."

"I can see that. I think that's great, Seth." And so different from her career, where she sat at a desk and crunched numbers every day. "Is that why you were in Afghanistan?"

"No. Well, sometimes." Seth shifted behind her. "C-17 pilots aren't typically sent to Afghanistan. What I did there was somewhat of an aberration from my normal duties."

"What did you do there, then?"

"I was there as part of a planning cell," he said after a brief hesitation. "We were tasked with setting up and expediting the transport of troops and supplies, as this particular area had faced some problems. Due to the extenuating issues, we were also tasked to develop procedure for and open communication with…a certain section of the local population."

"That sounds interesting." But also, Rebecca guessed, risky. Shivering, she recalled something Seth had said months ago. "In October, you mentioned you were here to recoup from a mission. What happened?" Every part of Seth's body that touched hers tensed. "Maybe I shouldn't have asked—"

"It's okay." He exhaled a short, sharp breath. "Several of us had to go off base to meet with a local leader. We'd made the trip before without incident," he said in a methodical, almost mechanical beat that somehow chilled Rebecca another degree. "But this time…"

Now, she *knew* she didn't want to hear this. But she *needed* to. "Go on."

"The vehicle ahead of mine was struck by an improvised explosive device. An IED, Becca. We suffered injuries and one fatality." Seth pushed out another breath, this one long and agonized. "In October, before I came here, I attended a funeral."

"I'm sorry." Tears sparked behind Rebecca's eyes. He'd never said one word about this to her. "So you were friends with…with—?"

"It's different over there." Seth braced his hands on the blanket. "The folks you work with, eat with, hang out with everyday, become a family. Even those you might not like so well under normal circumstances become important. We're all there for the same reason. When one of us… When we lose one, it's like having your own heart ripped out. It's always hard. It's always *wrong* even if what you're there for is *right*."

"You *were* friends, weren't you?" An old sadness welled within Rebecca, along with new grief for Seth. "What was his name?"

"Rick," Seth said thickly. "And yeah, we were friends."

"You haven't mentioned him." Of course, she hadn't talked

about Jesse, either. Not until he was brought into the open by her sister. "How come?"

"I don't know." Seth tensed again. "Maybe I've gotten really good at compartmentalizing my life and the different roles within my life. I think about him, though. Not as much as right after it happened, and not obsessively, but he's still in my head."

"Of course he is." Rebecca understood that completely. She also understood Seth's vehicle could have been struck by the IED. "But doesn't the way Rick died make you angry?"

"I'm not happy about it, Becca. He was my friend, and yeah, I wish what happened hadn't. But I remind myself he was doing what he wanted to do." A rough-around-the-edges laugh emerged. "And hell, Rick would hate any of us getting sappy. He'd want to know if we accomplished what we set out to, and then he'd clap each of us on the back and say, 'Carry on!' That was Rick. That's what I think about."

"But it could have been you," she said, her grief spilling out. "*You* could have been in that vehicle that day. Or another day. Or—" She stopped, caught her breath and resituated herself, attempting to alleviate the discomfort in her back. "You were in a place where you could have been hurt…killed at almost any given moment. Am I wrong?"

"The majority of the time, I was in fairly safe conditions."

"Seth, come on."

"I suppose you're right," he said flatly. "Anything could have happened."

His response burned into her like acid, but she'd known the truth before she asked. If she hadn't wanted to hear, then she should've kept her mouth shut.

Hating herself for pushing the topic, but unable to stop the words from pouring out, she asked, "Is there a woman somewhere whose life was shattered when Rick…when he died? Children? People who loved him and miss him?"

"Rick had a wife and two kids. A boy and a girl," Seth admitted quietly, almost with an air of defeat. "Yes, he had people who loved him. People who wish he'd made it home."

"But he didn't. And their lives are forever changed."

"Yes. But sweetheart," he said, "*I* made it home. I'm here with you now, aren't I?"

"For two more weeks. What will happen then? When you leave, I mean. What is your life like when you're not deployed as part of a planning cell?"

"I'll probably pilot a mission every eighteen to twenty-four hours." His body relaxed at the change in topic. "Every now and then, a longer mission will come up, meaning I could be gone from a few days to several months. There's training and simulations. Inspections."

"Several months?" Gritting her teeth, Rebecca waited out another painless flare of pressure. "How often does that happen?"

"It varies," he said, moving his hand to rub the swell of her stomach. "But if I decide…if all goes well, I'll be pinned major soon and my responsibilities will change."

"In what way?"

"Depends. Much of what I do will become more administrative. Meetings. Filling out forms." Seth cleared his throat. "If I'm made Assistant Director of Operations, I'll help oversee the day-to-day operations of the squadron. But the point is, and this is what I really need you to hear, my risk level is low and will only get lower as I rise in rank."

She heard him. She did. And okay, a lot of what he said made sense and eased her worries. But the fact of the matter was, "Your job, regardless of what you do in the Air Force, will always hold more risk than say…an accountant or…I don't know, a teacher. Even if what you're *doing* isn't all that risky, places you might be sent to could be dangerous."

"I can't deny that." Seth spoke in obvious aggravation. "I

wish I could. But...hell, Becca, a bus driver lives with more risk than a teacher or an accountant. Actually, strike that. I'd have to say that some teachers live with more risk than a lot of other professions. You *can't* wipe out risk. You *can't* live a risk-free life."

"But you can lower it," she argued.

"Sure," he agreed. "But to what extent? I'd rather do what I love than lock myself in a room afraid of the world. Bad stuff can happen anywhere at any time."

She opened her mouth, knowing he was right but still intent on getting *her* point across, when her stomach contracted hard enough that she couldn't speak. *Hurt* enough that she couldn't think, either. All she could do was stay still and breathe.

"Um, babe? Your stomach is as hard as a rock." Now, Seth's tenor held equal amounts of concern and curiosity. "Is this one of those practice contractions we learned about?"

Sickening fear and worry crawled into Rebecca's throat, almost choking her. "I thought so at first, when it all started. But now...now, I think maybe—just maybe—I'm in labor."

"What do you mean 'when it all started'? How long have you been having contractions, Rebecca?" Seth barked in a take-charge sort of way. "When did they start?"

"Earlier." Lifting her hand, she waved it vaguely. "Over dinner, or right before. I've had back pain all day...so it's unclear when this started. None of the contractions hurt until that one."

"Uh-huh. What happened to telling me the instant you weren't okay?" Both of his hands were on her stomach now. "Would you say you're having more than four contractions per hour?"

"I didn't think I wasn't okay! And...um. God, I think so." Crap. Just *crap!* "Yes. More than four."

"You didn't think, not even once, that perhaps you should

mention this to me?" he asked in a near-growl. "Perhaps while we ate dinner, or when we left the restaurant, or when we took a leisurely stroll through the friggin' park?"

His words and his tone began an indignant brew of mad and panic in her belly. What did he think? That she'd done this on purpose?

"Hello? Are you serious? I'm the one who might be in labor here, bucko. Not you. So I don't know why you're upset with *me,* but all I was doing was trying to figure out what your life is normally like. And you know what? I'm sorry if this inconveniences you, but I certainly didn't plan it, and… and…dammit! My back hurts."

She sort of whimpered that last part.

"Shh, sweetheart. I'm shocked, is all. I didn't mean to upset you." Seth moved so fast, her brain didn't grasp his actions until he stood with her in his arms. *How* did he do that? "It'll all be okay. I promise."

"Maybe this isn't labor!" she half hollered, half moaned as Seth strode across the grass. "I could be wrong. I *have* to be wrong. We have four more weeks and I haven't childproofed. We don't have a name." Grabbing Seth's collar, she tugged. Hard. Hard enough he stopped to stare at her. "Our daughter *needs* a name. She needs a safe place to live and she needs a name. This isn't supposed to happen this way!"

And that was definitely a wail. Apparently, she'd turned into a crazy woman. An angry, whimpering, wailing insane person. *Dignity,* she told herself, *conduct yourself with dignity.*

"She won't be born walking. There's time enough to choose a name and deal with childproofing," Seth said calmly and clearly with his eyes steadily holding hers. He took off again then, keeping her tight in his grasp. "Right now, though, if you don't mind and if there isn't somewhere else you have to be, I'd like to get you to the hospital."

"The hospital is a fantastic idea," she said, trying on the dignity thing for size. "Intelligent and well-thought out, considering the circumstances. You're good under pressure." Another breath-stealing contraction rippled through her abdomen. Forget dignity. Wailing was absolutely where it was at. "Why now? Why is she coming now when I'm not ready?"

"Perhaps our daughter is impatient to meet us." Seth smoothly deposited Rebecca on a park bench and wrapped the blanket around her shoulders.

At that juncture, two very important facts materialized in Rebecca's brain. One, her teeth were chattering and she hadn't noticed until that second. And, "Why am I on a bench? I like the hospital idea, Seth. I *love* that idea. Let's go that route."

Kneeling down in front of her, so they were face-to-face, Seth grasped both of her hands. "Listen to me, babe. I need to bring the car closer, so you don't have to walk three blocks. And getting the car on my own will be quicker than if I carry you the whole way. But to do this, I need to leave you alone. I promise I'll be fast. Will you be okay?"

Rebecca looked at him, this man she loved, who made her heart pound and her soul hunger and her body melt. A man she was considering changing every aspect of her life in order to be with. And as she stared at this man, at Seth, two more important facts materialized.

The first of which was the plain and simple truth that he had lost *his* mind. The second was that she was going to strangle him. Seriously, God help her, *strangle* him.

"Don't you dare," she whispered. "Don't you dare leave me here, alone, while you go for a jog through the freaking park to get the car. I would rather walk…crawl…*slither* behind you than be left sitting here on a bench while this baby is set on being born." One breath in, another out. "And I'll have you know that this, Seth, *this* is a very *bad* idea. Why, you—"

His lips landed on hers in a hard, fast kiss. "You're right, sweetheart. Message received." Seth hefted her up, first to her feet, and then back into the safety of his arms. "I'm a Class A idiot for even suggesting something so ludicrous. I won't leave your side for a minute."

"That's better," she murmured, curling into his chest, feeling one hundred percent more secure. "I didn't mean to sound so harsh, but honestly, what were you thinking?"

"I'm not sure," he said as he took off in a fast walk. "But it's a wonderful thing that *you* can think so logically at a time like this. Why, without you, I'd be a total mess."

"Are you being sarcastic?" she asked suspiciously. "Because—" A tight, heavy force descended, hardening her stomach and spreading through her back. "Go faster," she begged. "This isn't the time for dawdling."

"See, darlin'?" Seth's arms closed in protectively as he picked up speed. "Without advice like that, I might have stopped for coffee."

Seth leaned against the wall outside of Rebecca's hospital room, gave in to his liquid knees and slid down until his rear met the floor. Everything had happened so fast. When they arrived at the hospital last night, he'd been positive their baby was on her way into the world.

And, okay, she absolutely had been.

But a quick conference with Rebecca's doctor highlighted the risks for a late preterm baby. While the risks were low, an infant's lungs weren't fully developed at thirty-six weeks gestation. The baby would have less fat than at full-term, possibly making it difficult for her to stay warm. She also might struggle with breast- or bottle-feeding.

Since Rebecca's amniotic sac hadn't ruptured, and every day they could hold off birth meant more time for the baby's lungs to mature, the doctor's advice was to attempt halting labor. It hadn't been hard to agree. Because, frankly, Seth didn't care about how low the damn risk was…if they could make that risk lower, he was all for it.

This was his child. And nothing mattered more than giving her the best possible start in the world. The doctor immediately started the meds via Rebecca's IV. Within an hour, the contractions had significantly slowed. Within three, they'd stopped. Somewhere around the five-hour mark, Rebecca had fallen asleep.

For a long while, Seth couldn't force himself to move away from Rebecca's side. So he stayed in the room, listened to his daughter's soft, rhythmic, *reassuring* heartbeat through the fetal monitor and watched over Rebecca while she slept.

That had lasted several hours. Until, seemingly out of nowhere, everything closed in on him fast. The panic and fear and worry. The frustration of not being in control, of not being able to do a damn thing but *wait,* pooled in his gut and blazed through his veins. His muscles ached with the pain of it, his body shook from the shock of it and damn if he wasn't afraid he might just puke all of that negative, useless emotion out in an embarrassing display of weakness.

So he'd stalked the hospital hallways, looked at the newborns through the viewing window and paced some more. Now, burned out and a good dozen steps beyond exhausted, Seth sat on the floor outside of Rebecca's room, and wondered what the hell he was going to do.

In the crux of a situation, *his* decision had been to take the road with the least amount of risk possible for someone he loved. For the first damn time, he really understood Rebecca's side of things. And while he would never agree that keeping him out of his child's life was a good decision, he clearly saw what had motivated her to make the attempt.

He'd already forgiven her. This understanding should have set him completely free. Instead, it had tied him up in hard, impenetrable knots.

Because while he'd started thinking about changing his life for Rebecca, he'd held on to his hope that she'd change hers for him. Maybe he even thought she owed that to him, for what she'd tried to do. But dammit, he *couldn't* feel that way now because he *understood*.

His original ten-year commitment with the Air Force expired in about three months. What Rebecca didn't know, what he hadn't told her, was that as early as mid-September, he could be free and clear of the risk that so frightened her.

Or he could stay on for pretty much as long as he liked. Or he could follow through on what his plan had always been, the plan he still *wanted* to put into motion: take the pilot bonus, which would give him a nice chunk of change for an additional five-year commitment to continue doing what he was meant to do. So, yeah, he had choices.

He had the power to give Rebecca what she wanted. Probably, Seth admitted to himself, the same exact choice his family would prefer. But the dark truth lurking in Seth's soul was that he wanted it all: the woman, the child *and* the career he loved.

Which sort of made him a selfish bastard, didn't it?

Chapter Eleven

Thursday afternoon found Rebecca propped up in her bed with a pile of magazines on her left, a stack of baby books on her right, a whistle—yes, an actual bring-to-your-lips-and-blow whistle—and her cell phone in easy reach. Honestly, she was surprised Seth hadn't given her a walkie-talkie and a bell—no, make that a horn—as well.

She'd been home for slightly over forty-eight hours, and in that time, Seth hadn't relaxed once. Heck, as far as she knew, he hadn't slept, either. Mostly, he hovered and paced.

Right now, pacing seemed to be his activity of choice.

With a noiseless sigh, she watched him—his spine ramrod straight, his shoulders stiff, and his jaw hard—stride from one bedroom wall to the other. Back and forth he went, moving fast enough that his faded jeans and cotton T-shirt were a blur of soft blue and smoky gray.

Not an altogether bad way to pass the time, seeing how Seth was very nice to look at, especially in jeans and a T-shirt that hugged his form in all the right ways. But the severe, intense nature of his nonstop motion was beginning to wear on her.

Every time she attempted to discuss anything remotely serious, he cut her off and changed the subject. Probably to keep her stress level low, as the doctor had instructed. Unfortunately, the longer this continued, the more stressed Rebecca became.

She wanted *her* Seth back, so they could work through this together as a team. She also wanted to continue their conversation from Saturday night, maybe even begin to discuss ways they might be able to blend their lives. Well, if he still wanted to. Regardless, none of this would happen while he viewed her as an invalid who required coddling.

Cuddling, on the other hand, she'd be good with. Great, even.

Except... Well, there wasn't much of that happening, either. From the moment she woke up in the hospital on Sunday, he'd only touched her when necessary. And yeah, she supposed that was wearing on her as much as the other. Maybe more.

Seth came to a sudden halt in front of her closet and stood there for a second as if contemplating his next action. Whipping open the door, he dragged out her overnight bag, which was now packed and ready to go. *That* was the first task he'd taken on Tuesday, after ascertaining Rebecca hadn't gone into labor during the *slow* journey home from the hospital.

The man had driven as if he'd had a pile of C-4 in the trunk of his car. Whenever the tires rolled over a bump, he'd squeeze the steering wheel hard enough to whiten his knuckles.

She watched him then as she did now: in curious silence. Unzipping the bag, he took a quick inventory before stomping to her dresser, where he shoved a pair of socks in with the other packed clothing and supplies. Okay, he wanted her feet to stay warm. That was nice.

Heaving a breath, Seth zipped the bag and twisted to face her with an expression of pure, stubborn determination. A small muscle tensed, and then flicked, in his jaw. *Oh, dear.*

"What are you doing, Seth?" she asked, although she sensed she already knew.

"I'm returning you to the hospital," was his gruff, no-nonsense reply.

"I am not a defective blender," she pointed out, going for light and teasing. "And sorry, but you can't trade me in for another model."

"This isn't a joke, Rebecca. You belong in the hospital."

"If that was the case, the doctor wouldn't have sent me home." Not only a perfectly valid argument, but the absolute truth. "I haven't had a single contraction."

His eyebrows drew together to form a dark, grim line. "You're on bed rest."

"As you are aware, I am not on *complete* bed rest," Rebecca said primly, knowing if she didn't get through to him, she would, indeed, be on her way to the hospital. "I'm allowed limited walking, bathroom breaks and showers. This is more like taking it easy!"

In two days, Rebecca would reach their first goal of thirty-seven weeks. In nine days, she'd hit the thirty-eight week mark, which was their ultimate goal. Of course, Seth left Portland in *seven* days, so between him and the baby, she had plenty of days to fixate on.

"*Any* type of bed rest proves there is reason for concern." Seth resumed his pacing, causing her overnight bag to slap against his denim-covered thigh in soft thumps. "To my frame of mind, that means you should *still be in the damn hospital!*"

"Your frame of mind is wrong. Sweet, but wrong." She took a deep, fortifying breath. "Concern isn't *cause* and until there is cause, I'm not going to the hospital. So you might as well stop your pacing and put my bag back in the closet."

His entire body jerked to a stop. "Rebecca," he said, his voice somehow soft and dangerous all at once. "I don't like this."

"That makes two of us," she said. "This wasn't my plan."

"Maybe not, but *this* is the reality of the situation." He turned then, to look at her, and the weight of responsibility hung fiercely in his gaze. "Anything could happen at *any* second."

And didn't those words sound familiar? "True, but at the moment, I'm fine. Let's not borrow trouble." Desperate to distract Seth, to lighten the tension bobbing between them, she reached for the baby-name book. "Come sit with me and help me find a name. Please?"

"*Anything* can happen," he repeated, not to be deterred. "And when something *does* happen, my *strong* preference is to be at the hospital. Where there are doctors and nurses and fetal monitors! I would very much like to go there now, Rebecca."

"No, thank you," she said as sweetly as possible. "I'm happy being home."

His jaw hardened another fraction. "I don't know how to deliver a baby."

"You won't have to deliver our baby."

A calculating gleam entered his eyes. "Tapioca pudding! You loved the pudding there," Seth coaxed in a voice that in no way mirrored his oh-so-severe expression. "Said it reminded you of being in your grandmother's kitchen when you were little. Remember?"

"Yes, but—"

"If you'll stop being so contrary," he said, taking one long step forward, "I'll make sure you have as much of that pudding as you want."

"You're adorable." And cute, thinking pudding would be enough to sway her. "But I can wait for the tapioca until I actually need to go to the hospital. If you like, though, you go on ahead." For the hell of it, she batted her eyelashes. "I'll let you know when I'm on my way."

"That isn't funny," he all but snapped.

"Oh, come on. It's a little funny."

"Rebecca," he said, scrubbing his free hand over his face.

"Yes, Seth?"

"You're being obstinate and willful, and I *am* taking you to the hospital."

He came toward her, and being well-aware of how easily and speedily he could lift her in his arms, she did the only thing that occurred to her. She grabbed the whistle and blew three times in quick, ear-blasting succession.

That, she was relieved to see, stopped him in his tracks.

"I think," she said calmly, "it's time for us to talk."

"Are you in labor?" he demanded.

"Nope," she said, still aiming for calm and sweet, even though that whole want-to-strangle-him sensation was coming over her again. "Zero contractions."

"You blew the whistle. I told you to blow the whistle only if you were in labor."

Had he? "I'm sorry, but this was an emergency. I had to get your attention before you tucked me away in your car for another long, slow drive to a place I don't need to be just yet." Because he looked *so* darn worried, she added, "I promise you I am not in labor."

"Uh-huh. You weren't aware you were in labor the last time, or have you forgotten that?"

"I haven't forgotten. But now, I know what to expect." Frustration started a low burn deep in her belly. "Maybe you shouldn't be the person to stay with me. Maybe we should call my mom or Jocelyn, and you should go back to your parents' house."

Crap. The second Rebecca said the words, she wished she could take them back.

"I see." Heavy lines creased Seth's forehead and his shoulders slumped forward. Letting go of the overnight bag, he sat in the chair he'd put by her bed. "Do you want me to leave?"

No. Never. "If the next seven days are going to be a repeat of the past two, then yes."

Confusion clouded his features. "All I'm trying to do here is take care of you."

"I know. And I love y—" She clamped her jaw shut even as her cheeks grew hot at what she'd almost revealed. "I love *that* you want to take care of me. But Seth, you're either hovering or pacing or asking if I've had any contractions. This morning, you stood inches from the curtain while I showered, and the one time I suggested going downstairs to the sofa, you said—"

"That you were on 'bed rest' not 'sofa rest.' I'm...hell." He shook his head in dismay. "I've been mother-henning you to death, haven't I?"

"*My* mother could learn from you, and that's saying something."

"I'm sorry." Seth cracked a small smile. "It isn't easy for me to admit that I can't fix this situation. I...feel like my hands are tied behind my back and all I can do is wait and hope."

"I'm doing the same." Thank goodness they were finally talking about this. "It's my body that decided to go into labor four weeks early. I can't change any of this, yet I feel...responsible. I keep wondering if this is somehow my fault. If, maybe, you think it might be *my* fault, too."

"Not even once." Seth swore under his breath. "I...ah... asked the doctor if sex could've brought on labor. She said it was possible, so perhaps this is my fault. If so, I'm real sorry."

"Wow. Your male ego hasn't suffered any, that's for sure."

At his blank look, Rebecca cleared her throat—loudly—and sat up straighter, ready to do battle. "You believe that every time we've had sex, it was all your doing? Because I don't remember it that way. *I* remember leading you up here more than once."

"Well, yeah, but—"

"There is no 'but' about it. Geez, Seth. I was a *very* willing participant." Rebecca arched an eyebrow at Seth. "I'm sure my doctor also told you that sex is fine throughout a normal pregnancy, which mine had been in *every* way until Saturday."

"She might have mentioned something along those lines." His gaze, steady and sure, met hers. Held hers. And damn if every inch of her skin didn't tingle from a mere look. "Becca," he said, in more a breath of air than anything truly audible.

And yet, she heard him. "Yes?"

"If I'm making this more difficult for you, I'll leave. No questions asked."

Bye bye, tingles. "If you want to leave," she forced herself to say, "you should."

"No. But I want to make your life easier. Not harder."

"You do, you are." *Thank you, thank you, thank you.* "If you could relax—" Rebecca squeezed her thumb and forefinger together "—just a little, then I'd be able to relax a little, too. So, less hovering and pacing. Less staring at me like I'm a bomb about to explode. And no more demands to rush me to the hospital when there isn't a reason."

"Yes, yes, yes and…no. I can't promise that one," he said somewhat sheepishly. "If I have reason to believe there's a reason *even* if you say different, I'm not wasting a second. We won't go through that again. Not on my watch."

Delicious humor bubbled inside. "You really don't want to deliver this baby, huh?"

"I really, really don't." Tension seeped out of him, to be

replaced by a teasing grin. He waggled his eyebrows at her. "What do you say, do we have a deal?"

Biting back a laugh, she nodded. "I say yes."

"Whew." Seth wiped the back of his hand across his forehead in an exaggerated motion. "Now," he said with a nod toward the baby-name book, "Let's find our daughter's name."

Happier and more at ease, Rebecca moved the stack of magazines to the other side of the bed and beckoned for Seth to join her. She expected he'd do so instantly, but he didn't. Doubt filled his eyes, that muscle in his jaw tensed and his shoulders stiffened.

The hesitation only lasted a few seconds before he slid into place next to her, but it was enough of a hesitation that she wondered if they'd really set things straight. Icy intuition prickled the back of her neck, and she came this close to asking if there was something else on his mind they should discuss. But she didn't.

Couldn't, really. Not when they'd barely finished climbing over one barrier.

"What about—" she flipped open the book to a random page and said the first name her eyes landed on "—Fifi?"

"Fifi Foster?" Yanking a pillow from behind his head, Seth squeezed it to fit between them. And then—*then,* he sidled away from her, allowing the pillow to fully expand, separating them by a good twenty inches or so. "We're not having a poodle, are we?"

She blinked fast and hard in an attempt to expunge her tears *before* they fell. He didn't want to touch her? Still? Obviously, that part of the equation hadn't been resolved.

"We're having a human baby," she half whispered. "No poodles. Promise."

"I was teasing, Becca. Here—" Seth pulled the book from her grasp "—we weren't to the *F*s yet, anyway. We stopped at Darlene."

"Oh, that's right," she murmured. "I'd…forgotten."

While Seth searched for the proper page, she tried convincing herself that there were a dozen possible explanations that made sense. For example, sitting so close to her furnace of a body had made him too warm, or he had a scratchy throat and didn't want her to get ill, or he still had garlic breath from the spicy sub he'd eaten for lunch.

All were logical. All *could* be true. Except…Rebecca couldn't shake the feeling that something a lot more serious simmered beneath the surface.

"Ah, here we go," Seth said, his voice breaking into her turmoil. "What do you think of Dawn, Deanna or Debbie?"

"Any ex-girlfriends with those names?"

"Well, there was a Debbie in Dallas…"

Rebecca laughed because she knew Seth expected her to. "I like Dawn, but it sort of makes me think of the dish soap. Deanna is a possibility, though."

For the next hour, they circled and crossed off names. They got through the *F*s before Seth decided he should make dinner. He didn't kiss her before leaving, nor did he wrap his arm around her shoulders for a hug. A pat on her stomach had been the extent of the touching.

Closing her eyes, Rebecca again willed her tears to recede. If Seth didn't want to touch her, maybe he'd given up on the idea of them being together. Forgiving her was one thing— and, honestly, more than she'd expected—but choosing to spend his life with a woman who'd done what she tried to do existed in a different realm of difficulty.

It was a lot, she knew. Maybe it was too much. Even for a man like Seth.

"You're cutting off the crust?" Jace asked shortly before noon on Sunday. The two brothers were standing in Rebecca's kitchen, and Seth was in the midst of preparing her lunch. And yes, he was, in fact, removing the crust. "Who are you feeding, a four-year-old?"

Oddly embarrassed, Seth shrugged. "She never eats it, so why give it to her?"

"Um…because she's an adult and can eat around the crust all by her lonesome?"

"It isn't a big deal," Seth said, doing his best to ignore his brother's sarcasm. After slicing the sandwich in half, he set the plate—which already held a handful of grapes and a few carrot sticks—on the tray. "I…ah…appreciate that you and Melanie came over to visit."

"Isn't a problem." Jace plucked a grape from Rebecca's tray. "We'd be here, regardless."

Seth nodded his thanks. "It's good for Rebecca to have distractions." For him, too. Every time he so much as glanced in Rebecca's direction, he had to fight the urge to haul her off to the hospital. It drove him nuts she refused to go.

"Is that why you're scheduling people in like this is a dentist's office?"

"Partially. There's some friction between Becca and me, I guess you'd say." Seth retrieved a drinking glass from the cupboard. In truth, they hardly touched these days. Mostly because of how fragile she seemed. "Having folks around makes it easier. I can get stuff done and still know someone's with her. So I don't—" he coughed "—mother-hen her to death."

"I can see you're doing real well with that." Jace shot an amused glance toward the crust-free sandwich. "What type of stuff are you doing?"

"Stocking the freezer with meals, washing the baby clothes, shopping for supplies." In other words, Seth was doing his darnedest to complete every last to-do he could think of.

"Must be difficult," Jace said quietly. "Knowing you won't be here right off."

"I'll be here often enough, just not nonstop." Since Seth and Rebecca weren't married, he wouldn't qualify for paternity leave. Typically, though, his weekends were free and he might be able to snag an extra day here and there. Regardless, a lot of driving loomed in his future.

At least until September. If he chose to walk away from the Air Force, that was. The more Seth considered the possibility, the more powerful his want to do just that became. When he actually envisioned taking the step, though, something held him back. An invisible wall that wouldn't go away until he and Rebecca really talked.

And, as much as he wished for Rebecca's input, he couldn't broach any of this with her now. She needed to stay relaxed, and discussing his career options or their future—if they even had one—did not equate to relaxation. So this decision was Seth's alone. He didn't have long to make it, either. Within a matter of weeks, the Air Force would expect to be informed of his intent.

Sighing, he refocused on Jace. "I'll be here," he repeated. "As often as possible."

"We'll all lend a hand, Seth. Whatever Rebecca might need."

"I'm grateful for that." Seth knew the rest of his family and Rebecca's would do the same. "So...um...how did Rebecca seem when you were up there? Were her spirits good?"

"That's a curious question." Jace narrowed his eyes. "Seeing how you're with Rebecca day and night. Don't *you* know how her spirits are?"

"I know how she is with me, doofus," Seth said, playing the aloof card with all his might. "I want to know how she was with you."

"Why? Worried about something?"

"Yes. No. Hell. Never mind." Delving into this conversation wasn't high on Seth's list. Jace would be more likely to rag him than offer anything useful. "Forget I asked."

"Too late. But she seemed okay."

"Only okay?"

"I'm not an expert on Rebecca's moods, bro." Angling his arms, Jace leaned against the counter. "We chatted about the lack of a name for your daughter. She mentioned the partnership thing at her work. Jocelyn moving to California at the end of the summer came up. Hmm. Oh, and she offered to help Mel out with wedding plans."

Seth wagged his head, as if shaking water out of his ear. "*What* partnership thing?"

"Uh…you don't know?"

"Would I have asked if I did?" As he pulled out a bottle of water and a lemon from the fridge, he said, "Just answer the damn question."

His brother flicked an invisible piece of lint from his jeans. "In situations like this, I've learned to ask myself, 'What would Melanie suggest I do?' And," Jace said slowly, "in this specific scenario, I am certain Mel would suggest I stay the hell out of it. I think that sounds right, so that's what I'm gonna do."

"That's friggin' terrific, Jace. *Now* you develop scruples?"

"Better late than never, right?"

"Doesn't matter. I can guess the basics." With a silent curse, Seth twisted off the water bottle's lid and filled the glass. "This is the third instance I've learned something important about Rebecca from a third party. Petty as hell, but I am sick and tired of being the last to know."

"Understandable. I wouldn't like it much, myself." Jace paused for a millisecond. Then, "But why would Rebecca reveal a secret to me? I'm the brother who's already ratted her out once. So I'm thinking this is one of those things that just didn't come up."

"That's a point." And it was, but Seth didn't find any comfort there. He cut a thick slice of lemon, halved it and stuck the wedge on the rim of the water glass.

Dammit, this bugged him. Probably more than it should, seeing how he had a secret of his own. Sure, his reasoning for staying silent might be solid *now,* but what about two weeks ago? What about when she told him about Jesse?

He could have told her right then and there that leaving the Air Force in short order was within his power, but he hadn't. So, okay, he'd have to work that one out in his head.

"I don't know," Seth said half under his breath. Using a trick he'd learned from a past girlfriend, he folded a napkin into the shape of a hat and added that to Rebecca's tray.

"You don't know what?"

"To do, all right? I don't know what to do." Crumpling his hands into fists, Seth inhaled a lungful of air and waited for the tide of panic to dissipate. Of course, it didn't. That sensation, in one extreme or another, was a constant nowadays. "There are choices to be made. I'm having a kid and…I'm so damn scared that something will happen when I'm not here."

"I'll be here when you're not. Or if I'm not, Grady will be. Or Mel or Olivia or Rebecca's family. I swear, Seth, I'll make sure she's never alone."

"Yeah, that would good." Emotion punched Seth hard and fast right in the chest. "That would be real good."

"I'm not the best advice giver," Jace said. "But I'll tell you this, you two need to talk. And you need to do so before you leave."

Unable to speak, Seth settled for a nod.

"Does she know you love her?" Jace asked. "If not, I'd open with that."

Aw, hell. "Am I that obvious?"

"Nah, but that tray is," Jace said with a slight grin. "In my experience, men don't remove crusts from sandwiches, slice lemons for water or fold napkins into shapes for someone they don't love." One shoulder lifted in a know-it-all shrug. "Generally speaking, that is."

Seth looked at the tray and gave a second's contemplation to tossing the lemon, unfolding the napkin and making a new sandwich. But why? "It looks nice, though."

"It does," Jace agreed without so much as a twitch or a chuckle. "Real nice, in fact."

Thirty seconds of semiawkward silence passed before Seth said, "I…ah…should take it up. The tray, I mean. To Rebecca."

"And I should get Melanie. We're meeting her mom this afternoon." Jace was almost out of the kitchen when he stopped and turned around. "If you need me, just holler. Got it?"

"Yeah. I…I got it." Feeling far too sappy for his *and* Jace's comfort, Seth pushed out a croaky, "Thanks, bro. Means a lot."

Jace nodded and climbed the stairs, in search of his fiancée.

Seth gripped the edge of the counter and attempted to regain his normal, steady equilibrium. The way he'd behaved lately, he could almost believe in the scientifically impossible, that some of Rebecca's crazy hormones had leeched into his body. Never had he found it so darn difficult to reach a decision, formulate a plan and follow through.

He'd allowed his emotions to spin his head in circles… to *interfere* with calm, reasonable logic. So maybe Jace was right; maybe Seth *should* talk to Rebecca. Naturally, he'd have to proceed with caution. Upsetting her was unacceptable.

But if he laid out the facts in a clear, concise way, gave Rebecca the available choices and was then willing to follow *her* lead, he could stop *feeling* and start taking action.

Whether that meant searching for a larger house in Tacoma to move his family to, leaving the Air Force to move back here, or resigning himself to being a part-time dad, he'd accept Rebecca's decision.

And that would be that.

Grand Central Station had nothing on Rebecca's house. Or, for that matter, her bedroom. There were people here morning, noon and night. Between her family, Seth's family, her friends and even a few of her coworkers, Rebecca barely had a minute to herself.

Unless she was sleeping. Seth, she assumed, slept on the couch, because he certainly wasn't sleeping with her. She saw him every day, and yet she missed him. Truthfully, she ached for him. Of course, she kept that to herself. Asking for a verbal explanation of Seth's obvious emotional *and* physical rejection wouldn't only be stupid, it would be…cruel. For both of them.

Besides which, actions spoke louder than words. In this case, decibels louder.

Rebecca swallowed a sigh and continued ignoring her current visitor. Allison sat next to her bed, watching her with the carefully schooled expression of a mother who had things to say but was biding her time. Rebecca was lying on her side staring at her laptop screen, stuck in avoidance mode and pretending to work.

Seth… Well, who knew what he was up to. Probably more childproofing, which should please Rebecca to no end. But she figured that was *his* way of avoiding her, and that didn't please her at all. Under her mother's annoyingly steady appraisal, she gave up and powered off the laptop, shutting the cover with a snap.

"Oh, good. Now we can chat," Allison said in a bright, cheery voice that only served to worsen Rebecca's already sour mood. "I spoke with Seth when I came in. He's about finished with childproofing the kitchen. He said something about starting on the guest bathroom next."

"That's nice."

"He's also filled your freezer, organized the rest of the baby clothes and went on a shopping spree for any baby-related items you and my granddaughter might need."

"I know, Mom," Rebecca said with a noisy exhale. "I gave him the list of supplies."

"A little testy today, I see." Standing, Allison unfolded the afghan at the bottom of Rebecca's bed and proceeded to cover her legs. "Why do you think he's doing all of this?"

"Please, *please* quit fussing. I'm not cold and I'm not a child with the flu." Rebecca kicked off the blanket instead of succumbing to her basic instinct to scream. "He's doing all of that because I can't. He…wants to make sure we'll be okay when he leaves on Thursday."

Two more days until Seth returned to Washington. Two. More. Days.

"Well, yes. But have you considered there might be one additional reason?"

"He's avoiding me," Rebecca whispered. The hollow pain deep inside expanded and intensified with the admission. "He's avoiding me because he can't wait to leave."

Allison perched on the edge of the bed and smoothed Rebecca's hair. "Honey-girl, wherever did you get that idea? From where I'm standing, he very much wishes he could stay."

Oh, how Rebecca wanted to believe that. "He doesn't."

"He proposed to you," Allison pointed out, her tone soft and comforting.

"Out of responsibility, and he didn't propose. He ordered."

"What if he ordered you now?" her mother asked. "Would your reaction be different?"

"I…I don't know," Rebecca fibbed. She'd already gone

through the what-ifs, and if she could revisit that day, her decision *would* change. "I guess I wouldn't toss the ring."

"Maybe I shouldn't admit this, but I was quite proud of you in that moment," Allison said with a small chuckle. "The look on Seth's face was priceless."

Rebecca smiled but her heart wasn't in it.

"I think," Allison said carefully, "the reason Seth is busying himself with tasks that your father or I would be happy to complete is because he *can't* be here, not because he doesn't want to be here. I think he wants to feel as if he's taking care of you even while he's gone."

If Seth's behavior hadn't altered so significantly, Rebecca might be able to buy into that. "I doubt that very much."

"Why can't you see what I see?"

"Because I'm with him more than you are. You aren't seeing everything. *I* am."

"What I'm seeing is a woman with a broken heart. I've seen you like this before, Rebecca, so don't deny it." Straightening Rebecca's pillows, Allison said, "Does any of this have to do with Jesse?"

"Not really." Rebecca bit her bottom lip. "But I have been thinking about him. Comparing him to Seth and vice versa, considering how different my life would be if Jesse hadn't died. We'd be married by now. We'd probably have a couple of kids."

"You probably would."

"And this is horrible, Mom. So awful, but…" Closing her eyes, she pushed out a breath. Might as well say it all. "I think of that other possible life, the one I might have had, and…I no longer want it. And that feels wrong. That feels as if I'm somehow abandoning Jesse *now*."

With a voice formed from steel, Allison said, "You shouldn't feel guilty for moving on. Think of it this way, if Jesse hadn't died, you would never have met Seth." Soft fingers tilted Rebecca's chin, and as Rebecca looked into her mother's eyes, her own filled with tears. "This baby wouldn't exist, and you wouldn't be the woman you are today."

"I know. It's just…" Pausing, she tried to put her thoughts into words. "I don't regret loving Jesse. I believe we would've been happy, I really do."

"Oh, sweetie, you would have been. And if that life *had* happened, you wouldn't wish for a different one." Allison brushed a tear from Rebecca's cheek. "Your love for Jesse was strong and true, as was his for you. But why condemn yourself for a choice that wasn't yours?"

"Because I…I love someone else now." That was the first time Rebecca had uttered those words aloud. "I love Seth so much and I'm pretty sure he doesn't love me. So, yes, I feel guilty. I used to yearn for Jesse. Now…I yearn for Seth. Now, I wish that Seth loved me back."

"Well, of course you do," her mother said quietly. "And that's okay. I promise."

Drying her cheeks, Rebecca nodded, hearing nothing but conviction in her mother's words. "I guess I needed to hear that."

"Then I'm glad I said it." Allison pulled her into her arms for a tight hug. When they separated, she said, "Let the guilt go. There isn't any place for it here."

"You're right." Her daughter kicked, as if in agreement. "I know you're right."

One perfectly plucked eyebrow arched. "I'm always right, darling. Which is why you should believe me when I tell you that you don't have to wish for Seth's love. Unless I'm greatly mistaken, that man is besotted with you."

"Now, you're wrong." Even as Rebecca said the words, hope flickered in her chest, warm and liquid and terrifying. "You have to be wrong. He doesn't behave as if he loves me.

Not lately, anyway. And he hasn't once said he loves me. So why are you so sure he does?"

"I believe the question you should be asking, Rebecca, is what if I'm right? Are you going to let him leave in two days without knowing for sure?"

"He'll be back to see his daughter," Rebecca said stubbornly, far too afraid to put her heart on the line. "There will be plenty of opportunity for us to…talk."

"You're absolutely correct, dear." Allison picked up the afghan and shook it out. "I shouldn't push, and I know how you like to consider every angle. Take all the time you need."

Uh-oh. This was a mother-knows-best moment if Rebecca ever heard one. Bracing herself for the rest, she said, "Go on. Say it all."

"Take all the time you need," her mother repeated, refolding the blanket. "Why not, when love is as easy to find as a misplaced penny? And you're a lovely woman, Seth is a striking man. If you don't end up with each other, I'm sure you'll both find someone else." She cast an indulgent smile toward Rebecca. "Someday."

Chapter Twelve

"Failure is not an option," Seth chanted quietly as he paced the kitchen. "Upsetting her is not an option. *Hurting* her is not an option. Whatever she says, goes."

Pivoting on his heel, he looked over the picnic basket, fresh flowers and folded red-and-white checkered tablecloth. Everything was ready. Every item on his *and* Rebecca's to-do lists was checked off. The pantry was stocked, the childproofing done, the nursery in perfect order.

So what in the hell was he waiting for?

Every day for the past three, his intent had been to have this conversation with Rebecca. Every day for the past three, that hadn't happened. And now, dammit, he'd put it off until the last possible minute, and he was still standing in the kitchen procrastinating.

"Not cool," he muttered.

And it wasn't. Not when Seth should be driving out of Portland well before nightfall. He'd return by next weekend, sooner if he could work something out with his commander, but if he left without talking to Rebecca he'd regret it for the rest of his life.

His heart pounded erratically and his gut felt a lot like undercooked oatmeal—thick and grainy—and his head, well that hurt as if someone had smashed him with a sledgehammer. None of which mattered. All that mattered was getting this right.

Dragging in a mouthful of air, Seth gathered the supplies he'd so painstakingly arranged and walked out of the kitchen, only to come to a screeching halt at the base of the stairs. This emotional overload garbage was becoming...annoying.

Why this troubled him so much, he didn't know. He was, after all, an officer in the United States Air Force, and had worked damn hard toward fulfilling his goals there. He piloted planes and had successfully completed many a mission. Hell, he'd worn the sparkly-unicorn-girly shirt—*in public*—for the sole benefit of seeing Rebecca smile. And he *ran* three blocks carrying Rebecca in his arms, while she was in labor, and hadn't stumbled once. Not once.

So if he could do all that, he could absolutely do this. He *would* do this. Soon. Very soon, even. In five minutes, he figured. Surely in no more than ten.

After his knees ceased with their incessant wobbling, his palms stopped sweating and his heart climbed from his stomach back to his chest where it friggin' belonged, he'd be good to go.

Probably.

Fifteen minutes later, Seth hesitated outside of Rebecca's door, drew in a deep breath and mentally repeated his mantra. He could—*would*—do this. Right now. Firming his shoulders, he forced his gelatin-weak legs to move and entered the room. Instantly, his breath locked in his lungs and the heavy weight of emotion stung his eyes.

God, she was gorgeous. And she was...asleep?

Eyes closed and knees slightly bent, she wore a pair of comfortable-looking, pale khaki capri pants and a soft, buttery-yellow short-sleeve shirt. One hand rested on her now truly enormous stomach, the other loosely held the baby-name book against the bed's comforter. Someone, Seth noted, had painted her toenails a pearly pink.

Yup, gorgeous in every way.

As silently as possible, he crept forward and deposited his armful of supplies in the chair. Slicking his palms down the front of his jeans, Seth watched Rebecca and tried to decide how to proceed. Maybe this *wasn't* the best idea. Perhaps he should wait for this conversation until he was able to return. Except...as much as he feared what might happen, he couldn't wait.

He couldn't leave without at least *trying*.

"I'm awake," Rebecca said quietly, opening her eyes. "You don't have to tiptoe around me. I was just...thinking."

Action, his brain shouted. *Retreat,* his heart pleaded.

"Good," he said in his matter-of-fact voice. "I thought we'd share a meal together before Jocelyn arrives." With some flair, he grabbed the white-and-red checkered tablecloth and flipped it open. "You'll need to sit up a little more, darlin'."

With a wary-eyed glance, she did. He spread the tablecloth along the middle of the bed, retrieved the flowers and picnic basket, and crawled into place across from her.

"We're having a picnic?" she asked. "In...bed?"

He gave a stiff nod and went about setting the scene he'd pictured in his mind. His motions quick and efficient, Seth set the fresh-picked bouquet of flowers, hand-tied with a ribbon he'd found in Rebecca's hall closet, in the center of the tablecloth. Extracting the two already-filled containers from the picnic basket, he passed one to Rebecca and placed his in front of him. Silverware, napkins, and two bottles of lemonade followed.

"This is nice, Seth," Rebecca said as she opened her container. "I... You didn't have to do this, though. I know you want to stop by and see your folks."

"I wanted to do this," he said gruffly. "And I have plenty of time."

"Well, then let's dig in," she said, her gaze not meeting his. "Pasta salad, yum."

"Your mom made it," Seth admitted, working his mind around to how he was going to start saying everything he had to say. "And my mom baked the cookies. But...ah...I cut up the fruit. And...well, put all of this together."

"The flowers are pretty. Are those from out front?"

"Uh-huh." Why did his tongue feel as sticky as Elmer's glue?

They ate in silence for a few minutes, the whole while Seth's stomach churned and twisted and a weight as heavy as any anchor came to rest on his shoulders. For the first time in his adult life, he wished he wasn't in the Air Force. For the first time, he wished he worked as an insurance agent, or in real estate...or hell, at the McDonald's up the road.

"We don't have a name yet," Rebecca said after swallowing a mouthful of lemonade.

"I know. I've been thinking we might need to see her face in order to name her."

"I thought of that." With a sigh, she closed her container and leaned back against her pillows. "I'm sorry. You've gone to all this trouble and I don't really have an appetite."

"Wasn't any trouble." Seth pushed his fork around in his pasta, not feeling much of an appetite himself. Clearing his throat, he said, "Jace mentioned something about a partnership at your firm. I've been meaning to ask, but the past couple days slipped by without me noticing."

She blinked once, twice and her hand came to her mouth. "Oh, I never told you about that, did I? Dang it, Seth...I swear that wasn't on purpose. It isn't anything definite. Just a possibility the partners want to discuss after my maternity leave. And...I guess when we were together, I had other things on my mind."

"We've had a lot going on, Becca." Some of his frustration dissipated at the truth he heard in her voice. "That's great news. Being made a partner is a big deal, so you should be proud. Real proud."

Shifting slightly, Rebecca twisted the lemonade bottle's cap on and off. "It isn't definite," she repeated. "But of course I'm pleased. It's nice to know they're aware of how hard I've worked and that they view me as an asset."

And that right there, Seth figured, crossed off one of the options he'd planned on presenting. Why would she choose to relocate her entire life to Tacoma with a potential partnership looming in her future? Disappointment settled, swift and sour, but he set it aside. Hadn't he already known that option was pretty much out of the running? Yeah, he had.

Time to move on.

Be clear. Be concise. "Rebecca, there are issues I believe should be discussed before our daughter is born. Her birth will alter our relationship, perhaps cloud our judgments, which might then lead to poor decisions. I think," he said crisply, "the best method to avoid such a scenario is to go over our available choices now, while our emotions remain uncluttered."

With a mental pat on his shoulder for starting off so well, Seth beamed. That hadn't been nearly as difficult as he'd expected. The rest should be a piece of cake now.

Rebecca's hand halted. Her blue-green eyes darkened to a murky, stormy shade. "You put this picnic together to discuss our issues while our emotions remain uncluttered, before our judgments cloud, so we will be less prone to forming poor decisions? Do I have this right?"

"Yes." Pleased he'd related his thoughts clear enough that he didn't have to waste time explaining himself, he pushed forward to the next item on his agenda, which he'd arranged in his head like the many to-do lists he'd recently completed. "If you have no objections, I'd like to start with Jesse. Particularly, are you still in love with him?"

Rebecca gave Seth an inscrutable look. "I will always love Jesse, but I am no longer in love with him. I haven't been for quite some time." Her eyes sharpened and then narrowed. "Does this issue require further discussion?"

"No." Fierce relief blocked everything else out. Rebecca's heart didn't belong to a ghost. That was good news. "Unless you would like to elaborate," he offered.

"I don't think so." She angled her arms over her stomach. "Is there more?"

"Yes." Seth crunched his hands into fists to fight against the compulsion to touch her, hold her. Kiss her. Declare his undying love for her. That had to wait until he got this next part out. "I understand how your experiences with Jesse have...colored your view on being with someone who is in the military. So I have two options to present to you."

"Only two?" she asked with a strange, hollow quality echoing in her voice.

"Two," he said firmly, reminding himself that the third option was no longer on the table. "And I will accept whichever option you choose, Rebecca. Without question or discussion."

"I wish I could express how grateful I am that you've worked all of this out on your own, and all I have to trouble myself with is selecting an option." Rebecca spoke in a soft and sweet manner, but also with a slight nuance of...sarcasm? Nah. Couldn't be. "Why, this is almost like a multiple choice quiz, isn't it?"

Seth swiped his jaw, feeling the first prickle of uncertainty. "Maybe I should back up some and start again."

"Oh, no. I'm ready to hear my options."

Well, okay then. "Option number one is I accept your prior decision, I remain in the Air Force and I visit Portland whenever I can to create a relationship with my child. I will help out financially and in any other way possible. My family is here, so they will be able to offer the day-in, day-out support you might need."

Rebecca laced her fingers together and her eyes narrowed another fraction. "You've obviously given option one a lot of thought, and I do adore your family." A slight pause, then, "Now, I find I'm curious about option two."

Something wasn't right. Seth knew it, but he'd gone too far to retreat now.

"Option number two is I leave the Air Force when my ten-year commitment expires, which is in September of this year. I…ah…have neglected to mention this fact to you previously, for which I apologize." He sucked in a breath, and for some unknown reason, changed what he'd planned on saying. "I'll find a place to live close by, so I can be here for the day-in and day-out."

One eyebrow raised. "You can leave the Air Force in September?"

Seth nodded but kept his mouth securely shut. Why had he removed marriage from option number two? Because his stomach, head and every bone in his body hurt. Because… he was afraid. It wasn't too late. If she went that route, he'd simply slip the idea back in.

"If you stay in the Air Force, does that mean another ten years?" she asked.

"I have two choices if I stay," he said slowly, unsure of the current direction of this conversation. "Assuming I am able to continue to effectively and properly complete my duties,

I can stay on for as little or as long as I like. Or I can accept the pilot's bonus, which would require an additional five-year commitment."

"Hmm." Rebecca huffed out a short breath while blinking rapidly. "But my options are to *allow* you to remain in the Air Force but you'll visit whenever you can, or *choose* for you to leave the Air Force in order to move somewhere close by?"

"Correct." Pressure thrummed through Seth's muscles and his heart knocked against his chest so damn hard, he thought it might explode. "Do you have any other questions or...?"

If she gave him the merest hint of wanting more, he'd offer her the world. But he required *something* from her, some sign proving he wasn't alone in his feelings...that she also wanted the future he saw so vividly. In a moment of pure clarity, the invisible wall became visible. No wonder he hadn't been able to settle his mind on a decision.

He wanted the real thing: commitment based on love, on the knowledge that no other person would fit quite as well as the one you were with. He wanted what his parents and brothers had. And he wanted all of this with Rebecca, but only... only if she wanted the same. Without thought, he pushed his fingers in the front pocket of his jeans. Rebecca's ring was there, still waiting for the right moment. And yeah, he'd sell his soul for *this* to be that moment.

"No, Seth," Rebecca said, her tone flat and emotionless. "I don't believe I have any other questions. I...fully understand both of my options."

"Alrighty, then." A rock, hard and unyielding, appeared in his throat. "If you'd like to think on it some, we can—"

"I choose option number one," Rebecca broke in, her voice icy. "And as you promised zero discussion or questions, I believe we are done."

Her words, her tone, the tilt of her chin and the look in her eyes crushed every last bit of hope clean away. Unwilling to leave—*how* could he leave?—he started gathering the remnants of their dinner. "Of course," he said. "I'll just get all of this out of your way."

"Just leave, Seth. Go see your family...be safe driving to Tacoma." Averting her gaze, Rebecca let out a shaky-sounding breath. "But leave. Now, please."

"I'm not leaving until Jocelyn arrives."

"You can wait for her downstairs."

Not seeing any way around it, Seth rose to his feet. Never had he wanted to stay in one place so much in his entire life. Never had he felt so sick...so broken and bruised and beaten inside. He made it as far as the door before turning around. Rebecca sat with her spine straight and her hands glued to her belly. She stared out the window, so he couldn't see her eyes.

He really, really wished he could see her eyes.

A car door slammed from the street, easily heard through the open window. "My sister is here," Rebecca said without looking in his direction. "Now you don't even have to wait."

"You'll let me know when you go into labor, won't you?" He swallowed and felt his pulse jump in his neck. "If I can get here, I will."

"Uh-huh. Of course I will." A quick intake of breath. "Goodbye, Seth."

Arguments crowded his mouth, so many he nearly choked on the need to spill them all. But dammit, if nothing else, Seth was an honorable man. He told her right from the start he'd accept her decision, and that meant...hell. That meant it was time to leave.

"Goodbye, Rebecca," he said softly, every word a sharp stab to his heart. "I have simulations this weekend, but I'll see you next weekend. If not sooner."

Her only response was a flutter of her fingers as she waved farewell.

* * *

The tears began an entire millisecond before Seth exited her bedroom. Alone now, Rebecca allowed them to roll silently down her cheeks as she stared steadfastly out the window. From here, she could just see the trunk of Seth's car. From here, she'd know the second he backed out of her driveway and drove off.

For some inexplicable reason, she needed to see him leave. Closure, she supposed. Until he left, her stubborn hope would live on.

She brushed at her cheeks, smearing the tears across her face and into her hair. Sadness and pain and loss and sorrow mixed with the red-hot irritation flowing through her blood. With the precision of a brain surgeon, she focused on the anger, pried it loose and yanked it to the surface, so *anger* would be the emotion overriding all else.

Mad was better than misery. Mad didn't make her want to curl up in a ball and lock out the world. *Mad* meant she didn't have to acknowledge the knot of pain in the pit of her stomach.

Because...dammit! The very second she'd opened her eyes to Seth, to the picnic he'd planned, the pearl of hope in her chest had blown up like a big, fat water balloon. How else was she to feel but hopeful? Not only had he picked her flowers, but he'd tied a freaking ribbon around the stems. A romantic scene, she'd thought. Her heart had softened and warmed and silly dreams roared into her head.

But then, he'd ruined the romantic scene, the hope bubbling and percolating in her veins, by announcing they had *issues* and he was giving her *options. Two* of them. Both of which were about as appealing as...as chopped liver with a side of chocolate sauce.

"Uncluttered emotions," she whispered in a sneer. "Unclouded judgments."

Her temper growing, Rebecca egged it on by bringing his

voice to mind. That crisp, methodical, *military* tenor had set her nerves on edge the instant he started in on his…*options*. Right then and there, she decided she would never use the horrible word *option* again. Ever.

And of course, with the two opt…*choices* he'd bestowed on her, how could she choose anything except for choice number one? Their discussion in the park had shown her up close and personal how devoted Seth was to the Air Force. She refused to be the person to take that away from him. Under *any* circumstance.

What *she* wanted to know was what had happened to choice number three? Where had the idea of marrying each other and raising their daughter together…and *loving* each other gone?

Unfair, the voice of Rebecca's conscience whispered. *Seth never claimed to love you.* And there went her anger, swirling down the drain. Sighing, Rebecca acknowledged the truth: she couldn't expect Seth to offer her a lifetime of love if he didn't love her. That would be a lie and lying was bad. And really, she shouldn't have hoped so hard that her mother was right.

Oh, God. *Why can't he love me?*

A murmur of voices, too soft to discern actual words, filtered in through her open window. Seth's and Jocelyn's voices. The beginnings of panic, faint but irrefutable, stirred inside.

He was leaving.

Sliding to the edge of the bed, Rebecca heaved herself to a stand, her gaze planted on Seth's car. She pressed her back against the wall and, using the curtain as camouflage, peered through the window to the ground below.

Her sister hugged Seth tight, and Seth tugged a fading purple lock of Jocelyn's hair in return. Jocelyn stepped backward and lifted her hand in a wave, and Rebecca's panic intensified. A sob whimpered from her throat. Seth was leaving.

Right now. And there wasn't one thing in the entire universe she could do but watch.

The knot of pain in her stomach expanded until she all but shuddered with it. The emptiness of losing Seth was…immeasurable. Impossible. Her tears fell harder, running down her cheeks and dripping into the corners of her mouth, but she didn't care.

Why wasn't there an option three? *Why can't he love me?*

Seth opened the rear door and tossed his extra-large duffel into the backseat. Her mother's assurances pounded in Rebecca's head: "He's besotted with you," and "He very much wishes he could stay," and finally, the worst of the lot, "What if I'm right? Are you going to let him leave without knowing for sure?"

Oh, God. Oh, God. Oh, God. Oh, God.

Now crying with enough strength to severely compromise her vision, Rebecca viciously swiped at her tears. Her baby kicked hard and resolutely, as if…as if ordering her to get a move on already. *Now.* Before it was too late. Before Seth and Rebecca adjusted to this idiotic, lame-brained notion and made the mistake—the absolutely unredeemable mistake—of forming their lives around *freaking option number one.*

Okay, that was ridiculous. Once again, Rebecca was flat out losing her marbles. Because everyone knew a fetus, no matter how brilliant, wasn't capable of kicking out her thoughts for the world to decipher. But maybe…maybe if Rebecca had a sign—just one itty-bitty sign—that Seth loved her or even that he *might be able* to love her, she'd put her heart on the firing line. Was that too much to ask? One measly sign for such a huge risk?

Rebecca fixated her gaze on Seth, who now stood next to the driver's-side door. If he so much as glanced toward her window, she'd run with it. Well, she thought that would be enough to push her into action. He opened the car door and bent to climb in… Her heart crashed to her toes. Maybe the car wouldn't start. Maybe he'd back out and hit her mailbox.

Surely, either of those could be considered a sign.

For no reason that Rebecca could see, Seth suddenly stopped midmotion and slowly straightened to a full stand. His jaw jerked up, toward her window, causing her heart to float up, up, up and away. In what seemed to be slow motion, he brought his fingers to his chest and crossed his heart with an invisible X.

She melted. She froze. She stopped thinking.

He then lifted those same fingers to his lips and blew a kiss into the air. And dang if a warm summer breeze didn't drift in at that second and wave the curtain smack into her cheek.

A sign! This was a sign! Had to be. But…now he was getting in his car. He was leaving. No! He couldn't leave. Not yet. She had to stop him. *Okay, okay, okay.* What to do? Yell? No, he was already in his car. Moving far faster than she should, Rebecca stumbled around the bed, grabbed the whistle and put it to her lips. She took to the stairs, blowing the whistle with all her might and hoping—oh, how she hoped—Jocelyn would hear and somehow *stop* Seth.

Reaching the bottom of the stairwell, Rebecca waddled her way to the living room and nearly collided with her sister. The whistle dropped from her mouth to the carpet.

"Where's Seth?" Rebecca demanded. "Did you stop him?"

Jocelyn's green eyes widened in alarm. "Are you in labor? Should I call Mom and Dad?"

"No and no." Rebecca fisted her hands. *"Where is Seth?"*

"Uh…he just pulled out. Why? What's wrong?"

"Oh, God. No, no, no. I can't be too late," Rebecca half cried, half wailed as she tried to push around Jocelyn, who now had a death grip on her wrists. "Did he say he was going to his parents? Is he coming back here? Did he say *anything* about coming back today?"

"He is going to his parents," Jocelyn confirmed, the alarm in her eyes changing to a gleam of understanding. "If he's stopping here again, he didn't mention it."

"My phone! I need to talk to Seth. I need to ask him about option number three." Rebecca tried to free herself from her sister. "Why didn't I think of my phone before? I could have called him from upstairs and stopped him and—"

"Is your cell in your bedroom?" At Rebecca's frantic nod, Jocelyn finally let go. She took off running, saying, "I'll get it, sis. Hang tight."

It was going to be okay. It *had* to be okay. Bracing her arms around the bottom of her stomach for support, Rebecca weaved a jagged line toward the front door. She *knew* she was too late, but she had to check. Had to see for herself that Seth was gone.

And yeah, he was.

Trembles of disappointment and shock overtook her, coursing through her body and chilling her blood. Briskly rubbing her arms, Rebecca unsteadily descended the porch stairs and stared down the street. Too freaking late. And okay, she *would* see him again. Even if her phone call didn't bring him back today, he'd return by next weekend. If not sooner.

Somehow, though, that knowledge didn't bring her any peace.

Again, hot tears welled in her eyes. Again, she mopped them away. She *hated* being such a crybaby. *Hated* her complete loss of control over her own emotions. The last time she'd cried with such overwhelming pain had been when... when Jesse died. When the horrible realization set in that she would never see him or hear his voice again.

"This is different," Rebecca said into the air, her voice a tangle of deep sorrow and dark regret. "Seth *isn't* Jesse. Seth *isn't* gone forever. This. Is. Different."

Swiveling, she faced the house, her intent to somehow

calm down so she wasn't a fanatical freak of a mess when she talked with Seth, when she offered him her heart, when she—

Oh. The rosebushes. Seth's ring.

A sense of conviction, of *rightness,* came over her, pulling her inches away from the edge of hysteria. She had to find that ring. She had to find that ring...*now.*

Rebecca altered her direction and strode purposefully toward the bushes, now ignoring the tears that refused to stop. The roses were in full bloom, their fragrance sweet and strong, beautiful and alive. Small, closed buds and large, open blooms swarmed the bushes, filling the natural gaps, making it near impossible to see where the ring might have fallen.

In other words, her roses were *hiding* Seth's ring.

She planted her hands on her hips and considered the bushes. They might have to go. She might have to systematically cut off every last stem, flower, branch and leaf in order to find the ring. If so, she'd do it in heartbeat. Without pause or a flicker of regret.

First, though, she'd try a less drastic measure. After slowly and carefully lowering herself to her knees, Rebecca scooted as close to the first bush as possible and thrust her hands across the top layer of soil. She started in the front and worked her fingers as far back as she could, digging into the dirt, disregarding the rubbing and scratching of the thorns poking into her skin.

Every second that ticked by without feeling the smooth circle of white gold on her fingertips only served to heighten Rebecca's need *to find it.* Purpose became obsession. As she intensified her search, her movements became jerkier. And though she would've sworn it impossible, she cried harder, her tears now a never-ending wash pouring out and down in a saturating gush of too many emotions to name.

The idea that a happily-ever-after ending with Seth wouldn't—couldn't—happen *unless* Rebecca held the diamond ring in her hand fixed in her mind with an absoluteness she didn't question. Not locating Seth's ring was intolerable.

"Where is it?" she sobbed, pushing her fingers deeper into the soil.

Lost as she was, she barely registered the sound of the front door opening and closing, the footsteps padding down the porch stairs, or the stunned exclamation behind her. It was the pressure of a hand on her shoulder that alerted her to Jocelyn's presence.

"What t-took you so l-long?" Rebecca said through her incessant sobs.

"Your cell was kicked half under your bed, so it took me a few minutes to find it." Jocelyn rubbed Rebecca's shoulders. "But don't worry. I already called Seth."

"You called him? What d-did you say? Is he—"

"I told him you blew the whistle and he should return." Jocelyn's hands moved to Rebecca's upper arms. Tugging lightly, she said, "Come on, sis. Let me help you inside."

"Seth's on his way? Now?"

"Yes, and he wasn't that far away." Jocelyn tugged at Rebecca's arms again, a little stronger than before. "If he sees you under that bush, he's going to freak out."

"I need to find the ring first! H-Help me," Rebecca begged. "Help me find the ring."

"Okay, look. I wasn't going to tell you this, but I—" A screech of tires cut Jocelyn off. She pushed out a deep sigh. "Uh-oh. He's here."

Chapter Thirteen

The first thing Seth saw when he pulled into Rebecca's driveway was the woman he loved, the woman he *cherished,* the woman who was having his baby, half under a damn rosebush. The second was Jocelyn trying to yank her sister to her feet.

Perhaps *yank* was too harsh a word, but what the hell did she think she was doing? Actually, what the hell did *they* think they were doing? Had Jocelyn *not* listened when he explained that Rebecca's balance was off-kilter? Had Rebecca forgotten she was *in labor* and should not, for any reason, be playing with her damn flowers?

Furious, worried, stressed beyond belief, Seth exploded from the car and stalked toward the crazy Carmichael women—both of whom owned his heart, albeit in different ways—with the sole objective of corralling the situation before it swerved completely out of control.

"Jocelyn," he barked as he approached. "Go upstairs and retrieve Rebecca's overnight bag. It's in her bedroom closet.

Rebecca, darlin', I don't know why you're doing whatever you're doing, but you need to stop before you give me a coronary."

Neither woman responded to his orders or, for that matter, seemed to have heard him.

"Jocelyn," he said again, stopping behind her. "Will you *please* bring me Rebecca's overnight bag so we can go to the hospital?"

"She isn't in labor," Jocelyn said in a rush of anxious syllables. "She blew the whistle but she isn't in labor, and now I can't get her to go inside."

It was then he became aware of the low, keening sobs erupting in thready whimpers from Rebecca. His gaze dipped over her crunched form, noting how her back quaked with each crying gasp, how her pale arms, which were thrust elbow-deep into the thorny bushes, trembled as her fingers twisted through the leaves and flowers in a desperate and focused search. Oh, hell.

"I got this, Jocelyn," he said, jerking his jaw toward the house. Whatever was about to happen, he figured Rebecca wouldn't want an audience. "I'll take care of her."

The pixie nodded. Squeezing her sister's shoulders, she said, "Seth's here now, Becca, so everything will be fine. You'll see."

Jocelyn walked toward the house and Seth folded his body to kneel beside Rebecca. "Hey, there," he said cautiously. "Feel like telling me what we're doing?"

She shuddered out a long, choking sob. "Go away. Come b-back in...in an hour."

"I don't think I'm going to be able to do that, sweetheart." Reaching into the rosebushes, he gently gripped her wrists. "Why, if I had known how badly you wanted these bushes pruned, I'd have dealt with it for you. How about if I do that now?"

"I'm n-not pruning. Please, Seth. I need to t-talk with you, but not until…not until—" She bent her head as another series of suffocating sobs pushed to the surface.

God, he was dying here. With care, he pulled her arms free of the bushes. Scrapes and scratches were webbed from her fingers to her elbows, creating a canvas of raw pink nicks to tiny beads of red thinning into streaks of blood and dirt.

"You're *hurt*." Knots of torment and regret formed in his gut. "Baby, we need to go inside and clean these off."

She faced him then, her eyes puffy and raw with grief. Her breaths came in quick, shallow gasps that tore his heart into shreds. "No," she said, her voice wobbly but determined. "I'm not moving until I…until I find your r-ring. I have to, Seth. You h-have to let me."

"No, sweetheart, you don't." He gave himself a mental kick in the ass. Why hadn't he told her Jocelyn already found the damn ring? "You don't have to look for the ring because I—"

"*I* have to find it. *Me!* Not you! I th-threw your beautiful ring away like it was g-garbage, and…and I didn't tell you about our b-baby and I can't fix that, Seth." Rebecca's face crumpled as another heart-wrenching sob burst from her lungs. "I c-can't change that horrible, s-selfish mis…mistake but I *can* find the ring. *I can fix that.*"

"I forgive you, Rebecca," he said in a strong, clear voice. She *needed* to hear him, *needed* to believe him. "And I know you would've told me, even without Jace's interference."

With a start, Seth realized he *did* know that. Rebecca's heart was too pure, too full of love to believe otherwise. Okay, it might have taken their daughter being born for Rebecca to come to grips with what she'd done, to settle her mind on correcting her actions, but he held zero doubt that she would've picked up the phone and called him.

"You *can't* know that. I d-don't know that." Lifting her

chin in that stubborn, I-will-get-my-way-on-this-no-matter-what manner of hers, she said, "P-Please let me f-fix this."

Every molecule in Seth's body rejected the notion. Every part of him wanted to whisk her inside, clean her off and tuck her into bed. But dammit, he couldn't. He *had* to give her this.

"Well, alrighty then." Moving swiftly, he changed position, blocking her sight of the bushes to his right. He pried the ring from his jean pocket and hoping for the best, pressed it partially into the dirt under the middle rosebush. "I can see how important this is to you, but darlin', you're looking in the wrong place."

"What do you mean?" She wiped her tears with the back of her hand, leaving a trail of wet dirt and blood from cheek to ear. "I stood on the p-porch and threw the r-ring here."

"You have a strong pitching arm, so if I were to guess—" Seth switched positions again and gave the row of bushes a contemplative look "—I'd have to say the ring likely landed right here in this center bush somewhere."

"You think?" she asked even as she began to crawl in that direction.

"I do." Seth got out of her way and situated himself on her other side. Angling his head, he peered around Rebecca, in search of the ring. Ah. There it was, stuck halfway in the ground with the diamond clearly visible. Relief struck fast. "I'd start at the bottom and work your way up. Between your impressive throwing skills and…uh…the natural elements—rain and wind and such—it likely dropped clear through to the dirt."

Guessing she'd need no more than a minute—two tops—to locate the engagement ring, Seth used the time to calm his racing heart and regain his equilibrium. Not an easy task, especially when the facts of their situation hadn't changed. He still had to leave. There wasn't any choice there. He was due on base tomorrow morning, simple as that.

And the knowledge he'd return didn't alter how much he wanted to stay.

A squeal of pure delight drew his attention back to Rebecca. Her movements were hurried, as if she worried the ring would somehow disappear now that she'd found it. Grasping the band, she tugged hard, breathed in deeply and then turned toward him with jubilation and triumph sparkling in her gorgeous aqua eyes.

Opening her fist, the ring lay in her palm, none the worse for wear. "Look! I found it. I found your ring. I found it, Seth!" A smile as bright as the sun wove across her face. She clasped the ring tight and brought her hand to her heart. "*Now* we can talk."

"I am very happy you found the ring, Becca, and talking sounds like a fine idea." Seth stood and rounded Rebecca with one goal in mind. "However, I think we should—"

"No you don't, bucko," she said, scurrying out of his reach. Frankly, he was surprised she could move so fast. "You are not picking me up until I've had my say."

"Be reasonable. You're covered in dirt and your arms need tending to," Seth coaxed, once again readying himself to lift Rebecca and carry her off. "We can talk inside."

"You had your say earlier. Now, it's my turn." She held up her free hand and shoved it against his legs. Hard enough he *almost* stumbled backward. Eyes that no longer held a trace of a tear darkened and narrowed. "You made me quite angry, you know."

"Is that so?" His knees jiggled—just a little—at the quick shift in her mood. Deciding to play along until he understood why, he sat down. "How did I make you angry?"

"*You* picked beautiful flowers for me and tied them in a ribbon! *You* brought me a romantic picnic, which you served on my bed! And then...*then* you ruined all of it by giving me...chopped liver and a side of freaking chocolate sauce!"

She pantomimed gagging. "Do you know how disgusting chopped liver and chocolate is? Do you?"

He blinked in confusion. Flowers, *check*. Picnic, *check*. Liver and chocolate? "I have no idea what you're referring to. Perhaps you could...expand?"

"Oh, I'll expand all right. You gave me two options. One is stupid." She sneered. Sneered! "I withdraw my choice of option number *one* as of now. And option number two is... is *asinine*. Put them together and we have chopped liver and chocolate."

Ah. *Now* they were getting somewhere. "I take it you're unhappy with the options."

"Damn right, I am."

"I see." Rubbing his jaw, he tried to appear thoughtful. "Well, the problem here, darlin', is those were the only two options. If you're unhappy with both of them, I'm not quite sure where that leaves us." A solitary strand of hope shot through him. "Do you have a suggestion?"

"I'm glad you asked." Leveraging her hands on the ground, Rebecca pushed herself forward a few inches. "*I* suggest we add another option to the mix. Option number *three*."

"Three options? Interesting idea, Becca. I hadn't considered beyond one and two." Following her lead, Seth planted his hands on the ground and moved a few inches closer to her. "I am curious, though. What would option number three entail?"

"We'll get there, but first, I have a question for you." She crept another inch in his direction. "And I expect you to answer in complete and utter honesty."

He mimed crossing his heart.

For some reason, her lips curved into a goofy grin. "When you make a promise to someone, is your intention to keep that promise?"

"I never make a promise I don't intend to keep." He slid

forward, erasing the remaining gap between them. Now sitting knee-to-knee, he said, "Of course, I can see how in certain situations a promise might have to be reconsidered. Once all extenuating issues are known."

"Uh-huh." Rebecca wrinkled her nose. "Such as someone picking you up all of the time, whether you want to be picked up or not, and hauling you around as if you're a bag of...of—"

"Exactly. Or being called a surly name in tense moments."

An eyebrow shot up. "What surly name?"

"Bucko, for instance," Seth said with a light shrug.

"Hmm. I'm not sure I would describe 'bucko' as surly." Rebecca's lashes fluttered. "What about people who just show up unexpectedly...constantly?"

"Now *that* is annoying," Seth agreed, leveling his gaze with hers. She was, he admitted, a bit of a mess, and yet, so lovely to look at, his eyes could hardly see anything else. "But I have one better. What about a man who loves a woman with his entire heart, but is too damn stupid to tell her?"

One blink, then two, then three. "Oh, I can forgive that," she said, her tone husky and warm with a hint of a tremor. "But what about a woman who loves a man with all *her* heart, but couldn't find the courage to face a future with him?"

"Couldn't or *can't?*"

"Past tense," she whispered. "I'm so done with allowing fear to form my decisions."

"Now, sweetheart, this isn't something you want to tease a man with." He was somewhat dismayed to hear a tremor in *his* voice. "This is too important and—"

"I'm ready to discuss option number three," Rebecca interjected, her tone even and strong. Determined. "And I would like you to hear me out completely before you offer any opinions or ask any questions. Can you do that?"

Good thing, because with his tongue tied in knots and his throat closed tight, he'd be lucky if he could get a grunt out, let alone actual words. He nodded and gestured for her to give him the details of option number three.

"We will continue on as we are, with you in the Air Force and the baby and me living here."

At those words, Seth's back stiffened and his foot started shaking in agitation. How was this different from option number one? He opened his jaw to ask when Rebecca gave him a quelling look. Fine, then. He closed his mouth tight.

"You will stay in the Air Force until you and I *together* decide it is no longer a good fit for our family. As to the pilot bonus, we will also discuss that together. Do you understand me so far?" she asked in a crisp, precise voice.

He replied with a weak nod and leaned forward, every muscle tense, waiting for the rest of it to pour out of her mouth. When she was done, regardless of what she said, he was going to kiss her. And then, he was going to carry her butt into the house.

"Good. Now, my timing here gets a little sticky, as I'm not positive how long it will take for my house to sell or for us to find a proper house in Tacoma. Maybe a few months?" She brushed a clumped chunk of hair off her cheek. "I'm sure you're now wondering about the partnership *possibility* at my firm. The truth is, your job is far more important to you, to who you are, and my job is nice but it's just a job. There are CPA firms all over the country. I'm sure I can find a good fit in Tacoma. If you had asked, I would've told you that."

"Are you—"

"I am not done, Seth Foster, so you just *hush*." Fire lit her voice, her eyes, and warmed her cheeks to a rosy pink. And even with the leaves in her hair, the dirt on her face and a stomach the size of Mount Rainer, he found her intoxicatingly beautiful.

He parodied zipping his lips shut.

"At some point, and I'm not entirely sure when, we *will* get married. You promised you'd say yes when I proposed to you, and while this might not be the most romantic proposal of all time, this is, indeed, a proposal, and I expect you to live up to that promise." She winked saucily and he just about laughed. "What do you say, *Bucko,* will you marry me?"

Seth didn't answer right off, just pretended to give the question some thought. "You realize," he said seriously, "that once I say yes, this is a done deal. There will be no backing out of a wedding down the road. And once we are married, divorce is not an option."

Her shoulders firmed. "I am in complete agreement."

"What about the surprises? I like them, you don't." Seth scratched his jaw, still playing a man who had a lot to consider. "And darlin', I have to be honest…I *enjoy* picking you up and hauling you around. I'm not so sure that will ever change."

"Hmm." The corners of her lips quirked. "Well, we might have a dilemma, then." She opened her hand to look at the ring. "Such a shame, though. I had my heart set on wearing this."

"If you'd like to try it on…"

"If I try it on, I'll never take it off," she said quietly, contemplatively, almost serenely. "In case you missed it before, I love you, Seth. With all of my heart. And if you'll just say yes, I think we'll have a pretty fantastic life together. But I won't beg."

"Sweetheart? Look at me." When she did, his heart cracked in two at the love he saw there. Love she felt for him. "I say yes, Rebecca. I will absolutely, without a doubt, marry you."

Rolling to his knees, he held out his arms, wanting nothing more than to hold her. God, he'd missed holding her. She came to him then, this remarkable woman he'd had the damn good sense to fall for, and his arms wrapped around her, bringing her as tight to him as he could.

"In case you missed it, I love you, too, Rebecca. And I will love and care for you and our children for the rest of my life. That's *another* promise, sweetheart."

Again, her chin lifted and fire lit her eyes. "That better be a very, very long life."

"I will do everything in my power to make it so." Drawing her closer, he kissed her with a hunger no other woman had ever raised. Passion sparked, hot and fast between them, just as always. But along with the passion and the hunger came a bone-deep contentment at knowing that *this* woman was the woman for him. She was his and he was hers.

And that was about as glorious a gift as any man could ever hope to receive.

Breaking the kiss, he whispered, "I love you, Rebecca. Fiercely. Completely. But darlin', that compulsion is coming over me again and I am a weak, weak man."

"What compulsion might that be?" she asked with a breathy little laugh.

"I'm sorry, I truly am, but I'm going to have to pick you up and carry you inside. And I'm going to have to do that right now. I hope you understand."

And then...well, then he lifted the woman he loved in his arms, kissed her soundly on the mouth, and carried her inside.

Epilogue

Rebecca experienced her first contraction on July third at precisely 2:33 in the afternoon. A fact she decided to keep to herself until the contractions were either five minutes apart or she could no longer hide the pain from those around her.

She made this decision for one very important reason: Seth. He had two days off for the holiday, and would arrive at Rebecca's sometime the evening of the third. She very much wanted the man she loved, her future husband, to be present when their baby was born. So…she figured she'd hold off as long as possible and hoped like crazy their impatient daughter would comply.

All went well for a while. Neither Rebecca's mother nor sister noticed anything amiss. Seth's parents didn't, either, when they stopped in at four. Grady and Jace, her designated watchdogs until Seth appeared, arrived together at six, and that was about the time Rebecca knew she'd likely have to ask them to drive her to the hospital. Her contractions were eight minutes apart, dropping from ten in less than an hour.

By 6:30, pain and pressure stretched across her abdomen every seven minutes, by 7:00 she was down to six-and-a-half. Seth, she knew, was over two hours out, and as she sat in her living room with Grady and Jace, she tried—oh, how she tried—to act normal.

Unfortunately—or fortunately, as the case might be—Grady had gone through this before, and he began to watch Rebecca very curiously at the 7:13 mark. Her fault, she supposed, for stopping midsentence to suck in her breath while gripping her belly.

Jace, as she'd learned from their encounter in January, was also a very observant guy. When Rebecca's next contraction rippled through her stomach at 7:19, he noticed. Probably due to her tiny—really and truly miniscule—yelp of pain.

The brothers looked at each other and had some sort of Foster-mind-meld moment that somehow didn't surprise Rebecca in the least. Without saying a word, Grady retrieved a notepad and pen from the kitchen to track her contractions while Jace climbed the stairs and returned with Rebecca's overnight bag. Then, both brothers calmly and methodically retook their seats.

By 7:52, Rebecca's contractions were coming every six minutes. She was uncomfortable, overheated and heading straight for grumpy without passing go. Grady suggested they leave for the hospital and Jace quickly seconded that motion. Rebecca testily explained that she far preferred to stay home until her contractions were five minutes apart, and unless something really wonky happened, Seth would show in plenty of time.

At 8:04, Rebecca's water broke.

And okay, perhaps this fell on the childish side, but she was *embarrassed* to tell Grady and Jace. The idea of discussing something so intimate with either of them, regardless of how much she might like them, was too much. Way too much.

Except…well, again, both men had proven to be very observant. Another strange mind-meld moment occurred, and without one word of warning, Grady hauled her up in his arms and Jace grabbed a handful of towels and her overnight bag, and she was on her way to the hospital.

They stood in for Seth until he arrived, helping Jocelyn with everything from rubbing Rebecca's back to spooning ice chips in her mouth. Jace kept Rebecca entertained in between her contractions, while Grady kept her calm through them. One by one, other Carmichael and Foster family members pooled into her room and joined in the effort.

It was crazy to the nth degree, but it was also…warm and comforting.

When Seth flew into Rebecca's hospital room, his eyes wild and full of love—so much love for Rebecca—she *almost* forgot she was in labor. Well, until the next *kill-me-now* contraction rolled in. He held her hand, whispered words of love and support, found little ways to make her laugh and gave her strength when she didn't think she had any left.

Shortly after midnight, the nurse kicked everyone except for Seth out of Rebecca's room. With fireworks blasting outside the window, Grace—lovingly and appropriately named after her two uncles—entered the world. She was perfect in every way: ten fingers and toes, a *very* healthy set of lungs and dark blue eyes that Rebecca felt sure would one day be a matching set to Seth's.

Later that day, when the Foster and Carmichael families took turns meeting Grace, Rebecca was reminded again of the terrible mistake she almost made. Her daughter had grandmothers and grandfathers and uncles and aunts, all of whom would cherish and love her.

The circle enlarged by one six weeks later when Levi Foster, Grady and Olivia's precious and beautiful son was born. Rebecca cried when she met her first nephew, when she stared into his eyes. Connections were...miraculous. She was a mother, an aunt, a sister and a daughter. Soon—before the year was out—she would be a wife. *Seth's* wife.

And that made her one exceptionally lucky woman.

* * * * *

REQUEST YOUR FREE BOOKS!
2 FREE NOVELS PLUS 2 FREE GIFTS!

◈ Harlequin®

SPECIAL EDITION
Life, Love & Family

SPECIAL EDITION

Life, Love and Family

USA TODAY bestselling author

Leanne Banks

begins a heartwarming new miniseries

Royal Babies

When princess Pippa Devereaux learns that the mother of Texas tycoon and longtime business rival Nic Lafitte is terminally ill she secretly goes against her family's wishes and helps Nic fulfill his mother's dying wish. Nic is awed by Pippa's kindness and quickly finds himself falling for her. But can their love break their long-standing family feud?

THE PRINCESS
AND THE OUTLAW

Available July 2012!
Wherever books are sold.

This summer, celebrate everything Western with Harlequin® Books!

www.Harlequin.com/Western

HSE65680

*Harlequin® American Romance® presents a
brand-new miniseries* HARTS OF THE RODEO.

*Enjoy a sneak peek at AIDAN: LOYAL COWBOY
from favorite author Cathy McDavid.*

Ace walked unscathed to the gate and sighed quietly. On
the other side he paused to look at Midnight.

The horse bobbed his head.

Yeah, I agree. Ace grinned to himself, feeling as if he,
too, had passed a test. *You're coming home to Thunder
Ranch with me.*

Scanning the nearby vicinity, he searched out his mother.
She wasn't standing where he'd left her. He spotted her
several feet away, conversing with his uncle Joshua and
cousin Duke who'd accompanied Ace and his mother to the
sale.

He'd barely started toward them when Flynn McKinley
crossed his path.

A jolt of alarm brought him to a grinding halt. She'd
come to the auction after all!

What now?

"Hi." He tried to move and couldn't. The soft ground
pulled at him, sucking his boots down into the muck. He
was trapped.

Served him right.

She stared at him in silence, tendrils of corn-silk-yellow
hair peeking out from under her cowboy hat.

Memories surfaced. Ace had sifted his hands through
that hair and watched, mesmerized, as the soft strands
coiled around his fingers like spun gold.

Then, not two hours later, he'd abruptly left her bedside,
hurting her with his transparent excuses.

HAREXP0712CM

She stared at him now with the same pained expression she'd worn that morning.

"Flynn, I'm sorry," he offered lamely.

"For what exactly?" She crossed her arms in front of her, glaring at him through slitted blue eyes. "Slinking out of my room before my father discovered you'd spent the night or acting like it never happened?"

What exactly is Ace sorry for? Find out in
AIDAN: LOYAL COWBOY.

Available this July wherever books are sold.

Debut author

Kathy Altman

**takes you on a moving journey
of forgiveness and second chances.**

One year after losing her husband in Afghanistan,
Parker Dean finds Corporal Reid Macfarland at her
door with a heartfelt confession and a promise to save
her family business. Although Reid is the last person
Parker should trust her livelihood to, she finds herself
captivated by his silent courage. Together,
can they learn to forgive and love again?

The Other Soldier

Available July 2012 wherever books are sold.

HSR71790

Harlequin® Romance

THE LARKVILLE LEGACY

A secret letter...two families changed forever

Welcome to Larkville, Texas, where the Calhoun family has been ranching for generations. When Jess Calhoun discovers a secret, unopened letter written to her late father, she learns that there is a whole other branch of her family. Find out what happens when the two sides meet....

A new Larkville Legacy story is available every month beginning July 2012.

Collect all 8 tales!